THE CARN-EVIL WAY

R.R. HARROW

CONTENT NOTES

Please note: it should be assumed that basic horror tropes will apply. These include death, gore, and violence.

For a list of other potentially triggering subjects,

please refer to page 130.

This book is for those who believed in me.

Acknowledgements

I want to take a moment to thank my family for their support as I spent hours locked away in my office writing, and the awesome team at Graveside Press. Particularly my editor Kell whose patience, advice, and guidance continues to challenge me to improve my craft. And Hannah, who (aside from tolerating my endlessly awful dad jokes) has quickly become the kind of rare friend & mentor that you consider yourself lucky enough to find once in a lifetime. You have my eternal gratitude & awe.

SUPER HAPPY FUN LAND

Harper Valley, New York, July 13th, 2005

"Look, Mommy, a clown!" Joanna Whipple pointed out the window of her parents' truck as they rumbled down the long, lonely, forested stretch of blacktop known locally as the narrows. She excitedly pressed her pixie face and hands against the glass and stared as they passed.

The stout black-and-white-clad figure waved cheerfully, its mouth stretched into the most enormous, red-lipped smile she had ever seen. Its eyes followed as they sped past where he stood, the gust teasing at the bunch of shiny black balloons he held in his other hand.

"Shouldn't we stop?" Joanna asked as the funny clown got smaller and smaller behind them. "What if he's lost?"

"Who's lost, honey?" her mom, Mary, asked as she peered out the window, following her daughter's tiny, pointed finger.

She pouted. She didn't understand. Couldn't Mommy see him?

"The clown, Mommy, the clown!" Joanna pleaded. "It's getting dark, he's by the trees. What if he's all alone? What if he's lost? Shouldn't we stop to help him?"

"*What* clown, honey?" Mommy rubbed at the back of her neck. She twisted around to stare out the back window and then her daughter, frowning. "Joanna, there's no one there."

"We passed him by, M-Mommy," Joanna sniffed. "He was all alone."

"Honey, I didn't see any clown." Her mom looked at her dad, and he shrugged.

"I didn't see anything," he insisted, "and I certainly didn't see a *clown*. I don't like clowns." Daddy occasionally glanced back as he drove along. "They've creeped me out since I was a kid. My grandma had a collection of clown dolls, and they looked like they were watching me…"

"He was *so* there!" Joanna insisted as her imp-like face crumpled. Angrily, she crossed her tiny arms over her chest and stared out the window. Pointedly, she did not look to the front of the car as her mother cast her a sharp, hard look over the purple plastic rims of her designer eyeglasses.

"Joanna, you do not speak to us that way! Look, I'm sorry we didn't see anything. I think, sweetheart, that maybe too much heat, too much sugar, and way too much excitement at the carnival grounds today has your imagination running wild." Fighting back a yawn, she offered Joanna a weak, sleepy smile. "Mummy needs to get home, darling girl. She's exhausted."

Joanna groaned, rolling her eyes. "Why are you so mean? He was standing *right there* on the side of the road, all alone. What if something happens to him? There's nothing around here but trees. What if he's scared? He could get hurt; he could be lost."

"Frank…" Mommy looked at Daddy with a pleading sigh. "Help me out here."

"Joanna. There wasn't a clown on the side of the road, trust me." Daddy visibly shuddered, his smile-crinkled eyes flickering from the road to her reflection in the rearview mirror. "And let's be real, sweet beans, even if there had been, I wouldn't have stopped."

"Daddy!" Joanna gasped with shock. "You're bad! That isn't nice at all!"

"I'm not picking up stray clowns." Daddy dryly chuckled. "That's how horror movies start. But since there wasn't any clown there in the first place, *thank God*, no harm, no foul... Right, babe?"

Mommy let out a long, tired breath like she always did when she rolled her eyes at one of Daddy's bad jokes. "I'm not sure you're helping."

"Dang, Mary, I'm trying here." Daddy bemusedly shook his head. "What do you want from me, babe? Our kid imagines, of all things, a clown on the road at night. I hate clowns. You know that."

"You're the worst, Daddy. He was there," Joanna grumpily insisted, pursing her lips as she kicked the back of his seat to drive her point home. Good and hard.

"Joanna!" Mommy scolded.

"Hey!" Daddy chuckled. "Tone it down back there, munchkin. I'm just joshing with you."

"The poor clown." Tears welled up in her eyes. "He could die, and you don't care. Not at all. He could get gobbled up and no one would know."

Her parents exchanged looks. They didn't know what to say. They had that stunned look on their faces that they always got when their grown-up brains glitched out. As usual, they went quiet, driving on in silence as Joanna glared tearfully at the back of their heads in sulking silence, hoping they would apologize. When they didn't, she changed tactics and pretended to be asleep for the rest of the ride home. Or at least, that was the plan until she fell asleep for real. But before she drifted off, she heard something that made her feel even worse, something she hadn't considered to be possible until just then.

"Franky," her mommy whispered, using the silly pet name she had for her daddy, "maybe we should talk to Joanna's pediatrician if she's seeing clowns that aren't there."

Joanna felt a sharp, empty sadness about this. Mommy was always on at her about growing up, about how having invisible friends for tea parties and make-believe were things she should have stopped doing by now, as she was a big girl—and big girls had to like big girl things. But she didn't want to. The tea parties were fun, and besides, the clown wasn't like the tea party friends; *he was real.*

"Aww… Mary, lighten up." Daddy sighed tiredly. "She was at a carnival, had sugar—way too much of it—and has an active imagination. She's fine."

"What if the other kids think she's a freak or a weirdo? What if they bully her because her imagination runs wild? You know how mean kids can be. Our daughter is so tenderhearted, she couldn't handle that. It would break her. First grade isn't like preschool or kindergarten." Mommy sounded worried, but her words wobbled and cracked like they did when she was mad. Like *super* mad.

Daddy sighed again.

Joanna's head spun like a spiny top, round and round. It wasn't fun or swell like a game. It made her want to cry, and that only gave her a bellyache. First grade didn't sound nice. If kids were mean, she didn't want to go at all.

She wanted to have fun.

She wanted to play.

She didn't want to be bullied because she liked those things. And worse, she didn't understand why her mommy and daddy were still acting like she was lying.

The poor clown had been *real,* not a game.

Joanna was wide awake, and she didn't know why. She blinked at the glowing plastic star-spattered ceiling of her bedroom and tried to figure out what had woken her. She could have sworn it was a scream, long, shrill, and terrible. Like from one of Mommy's bad movies. The scary ones Mommy always said she was too little to watch. Maybe Mommy had fallen asleep again watching one? She did that from time to time.

Joanna listened, waiting for it to happen again.

But it didn't.

It was quiet.

So peaceful.

Daddy probably woke up just like her and turned off Mommy's scary movie so everyone could sleep.

Yeah.

That had to be it, Joanna reasoned with a nod and a sleepy yawn.

Joanna had been having a wonderful dream of a wonderful place full of colorful lights and big striped tents. There had been giggling, cotton candy, and the smell of popping corn in kettles. Laughter came from everywhere, like she was in some super fun place packed chock-full of kids. Someplace amazing, where the crashes, beeps, and whacking sounds of games and carnival music were endlessly echoing about.

She frowned.

It made her think of the clown on the side of the road.

They'd left him there.

All alone.

Joanna hoped he was okay.

She really, really did.

It was cold; she drew her pink princess blanket around herself as she looked at her clock. The little hand was on the number three, and the big hand was on the twelve. That meant it was early. Too early. She yawned again, wider this time—then heard a squeak.

Then another.

Like someone tightly squeezing a dog's squeaky toy.

Joanna had always wanted a dog, but her daddy had said it was too much work for her yet. He said puppies were a yappy, destructive, and expensive undertaking for the family and they made him sneeze. That had made her sad, as she'd always loved puppies. She thought about petting a golden retriever or black lab while it panted happily. It was a nice thought. But Daddy wasn't going to budge on getting her a puppy. Not until she was old enough to care for it properly, as he put it.

The squeaks came again. And this time she sat up, listening.

It was coming from outside her door, down the hall. One squeak, two squeaks, three squeaks, four, five squeaks, six squeaks, seven squeaks more...

As the squeaks got closer, she heard the *jingle-jingle* of a bell, like a sleigh bell.

She giggled.

It was a funny sound.

Her door groaned open, and a pair of white-gloved hands pushed it in as a red-lipped, broadly smiling, grease-painted face peered at her through the cracked door. Staring in at her, with wide, friendly, glowing green eyes that were darkened about with black makeup. His floppy pointy hat, like Santa Claus's but black and lined in red fur, drooped under the weight of its big red pompom that jingled like a bell with every move it made.

The clown.

Her clown.

Joanna's face lit up. The clown smiled hugely and funnily. His red lips split wide, yellow teeth shiny and bright in the glow of her nightlights. Joanna clapped as he danced in, his red shoes squeaking and the bell in his funny floppy hat jingling merrily away. His feet even left red footprints on her white carpet. It was so silly, like a cartoon.

He spun and smiled, and she giggled and laughed, mirth misting before her eyes. Like it was Christmas morning in the cold snow. Joanna's whole room quickly filled with the smells of buttery popcorn, roasting peanuts, and the sweetness of cotton candy.

"Hi, Joanna, pretty, pretty Jo-ann-y." The clown bowed to her like she was a princess and honked a horn he pulled from his pocket as he did. His voice was bright and full of things, like whispering behind his words, like jokes cracked in the dark. "We are Witherwix the clown, at your service."

She giggled.

"You are a very special girl." He pulled out a balloon and blew it up for her, then started folding and twisting. The balloon squeaked as he worked it, molding it into a floaty dog, and tied it up at the bottom so the air didn't escape. He then added a string. It floated overhead as he deftly tied the shiny red ribbon about her tiny wrist. "Witherwix heard you. You were so kind to think of the poor, sad clown as he stood there all alone. But fear not, as Witherwix is well, and all's well. Especially for you, pretty, pretty, perfect, Jo-ann-y. All kind girls get special treats and rewards, and as Witherwix said, you are a very, very, kind, special, special girl!"

Mesmerized, Joanna stared at her puppy balloon, wearing a smile from ear to ear as she watched it bob there over her head, shiny, black, and pretty.

At last, her very own puppy.

"Thank you!" she breathed as Witherwix danced a little happy dance for her.

"You are more than welcome, perfect, kindly pretty, Jo-Ann-y." Witherwix whirled, honked, and squeaked about her room. Tumbling, cartwheeling, and laughing so loudly that it was a wonder Mommy and Daddy didn't come rushing in with all the racket he was making.

He stopped, staring at her with his pretty glowing green eyes as he withdrew from his puffy sleeve a golden ticket, thick, metallic, and gorgeously gleaming like lots of super special things that she wanted, and her mommy and daddy rarely got her because they were "too expensive." Witherwix smiled so impossibly huge as he held the ticket out to her in his pristine, white-gloved hand.

"What's this?" She took it, holding it like a treasure in her trembling little hands.

"It's a most special surprise." Witherwix the clown patted her gently on the head as he stepped back. "You see, not everyone can go. *Oh no.* Only super special nice boys and girls get to go to Super Happy Fun Land. Where everything is a game, every moment is a joy, and every breath is full of laughter."

"That sounds like magic!" Joanna squealed with delight. When she looked at the gold ticket and smiled at herself, her reflection in the metallic finish smiled and waved back at her.

"Oh, but it is. The very best kind." The clown clapped his hands happily as he appeared before her, big and bouncy and smelling of cotton candy and all sorts of other treats. He beamed down at her, his broad, painted face like rubber as the red lips curled up and up and up 'til all his big yellow teeth were showing. Joanna snorted with squealing, delighted peals of laughter at the sight of that comically huge expression, because he looked all at once like a Saturday morning cartoon from one of Mommy's old VHS tapes.

"Oh, Jo-ann-y," Witherwix giggled and clapped his hands with such infectious joy that Joanna ended up giggling right along with him as he spoke. "It's marvelous. Super Happy Fun Land is a place of such wonders. Oh, such sights and sounds and tastes, oh what fun. It's a special, magical place where it's never bedtime, and it's always snack time and play time for all the best boys and girls. All the fun, food, and games are free… And no one is there to say that's enough fun, no more sugary drinks or sweets. Doesn't that sound simply wonderful?"

"Yes!" Joanna nodded, fit to bursting with excitement. It really did sound wonderful. His laughter reminded her of the laugh tracks from the old sitcoms her daddy loved so much. The ones with so many voices all laughing all at once at a terrible joke that her mommy would roll her eyes at. It made her feel safe, warm, and bubbly inside. Like all was right as rain and butterflies.

She yawned and blinked. She didn't mean to, but when she did, Witherwix was by her bedroom closet's puppy-postered door. When her eyelids had closed, he was in front of her, but when they opened a hummingbird's wing flap later, he was all the way over there.

"Oh, that makes poor Witherwix so, so very happy to hear. Please, allow Witherwix to reveal the way to Super Happy Fun Land for you, pretty, kindly, perfect Jo-ann-y." He opened the closet door for her with a bow, which was super funny. A game or a joke only a clown could make up.

Then it wasn't a joke at all; it was real.

Light, laughter, and joyous calliope circus music poured happily from out of her closet, where her shoes were all tidily lined up on the floor. Her clothes should have been in a neat row, dangling from their hangers from one end of her closet to the other… But none of that was there, though what *was* there made her tingle with excitement.

It was her dream.

All the wonderful noises of a circus and a theme park all meshed into one amazing musical note that called to her, beckoning to her, thrilled her. Her eyes went wide and sparkly as she gazed in wonder at the huge wide world beyond her closet. It was magical. There were roller coasters with the beams all lit up in rows of twinkling white lights. Movie theaters, entire blocks of bouncy houses, ice cream parlors, a Ferris wheel—tall and brightly lit in many colors as it spun happily around. Spiny rides and teacups, swinging pirate ships and flying saucers, arcades, and attractions, and all the best fun. There was so much she couldn't make it all out. It looked like years and years could be lost in the blink of an eye, just wandering through the colorful, noisy rows.

Everywhere she looked, strings of lights hung between brightly striped huge tents and stalls where children laughed and played games. They were throwing balls at stacked cans, whacking moles with mallets, shooting squirt guns at targets that made loud exciting races happen, and popping balloons with darts.

And, oh, the smells. It was as if all the best, tastiest things were cooking at once. Cookies, cakes, popping corn, peanuts, doughnuts, hotdogs, hamburgers, fried dough, funnel cake, and pizza… Her mouth watered to taste it all, and her hands itched to play.

"Would you like to come with Witherwix to Super Happy Fun Land? It's perfect fun for special, pretty Jo-ann-y?" the clown asked as he gestured at the door. "All you must do is walk through the door. That ticket is your pass, your invitation to play forever."

She approached the door, then paused as a jab of worry popped the balloon of happiness that she had felt blowing up inside of her heart, deflating it all at once as she voiced her concern to her clown, "Won't Mommy and Daddy miss me? Won't they be scared if they wake up and find me not in my bed? Won't I get in trouble?"

Witherwix laughed at this, and his laugh made her happy as he shook his fluffy white-haired head, making his hat whip about and its pompom bell ring and jingle while he smiled at her. "Witherwix promises they won't miss you a bit, perfect, pretty, special little Jo-ann-y. And remember, in Super Happy Fun Land, it is never, ever bedtime, so they will never, ever wake up to find you not in your bed. Witherwix is a clown, and whoever heard of a clown lying, right? Haha." He honked his horn to drive the point home with a goofy giggle.

She smiled and laughed with him, and it was wonderful. "Okay, will you walk me in?"

Witherwix grinned broadly at this.

His glowing green eyes twinkled merrily as he chuckled at her question.

"But of course, pretty, pretty Jo-ann-y, Witherwix is your friend, and your guide to Super Happy Fun Land. What kind of friend and guide would we be if we didn't walk you in?" He asked, while he exchanged his horn for a shiny stamper. "All we have to do now…is punch your ticket." He held out his free hand, and Joanna hesitated, for in that moment Witherwix's face seemed to darken. Like scary, stormy rain clouds drifting over a warm, happy summer sky.

Then it brightened again when she nodded.

Joanna handed it over, and the clown put her golden ticket in its place and squeezed his puncher. It clicked, and he handed it back to her with another grand bow. The stamp was a smiley face, with her name about it in a circle, pressed into the thick golden paper. Her reflection on its gleaming surface was smiling and pointing at the stamp.

"Keep that with you now," Witherwix advised in a silly yet serious tone as she stared at it. "You can't crossover into Super Happy Fun Land without your ticket. Are you ready to go, perfect, pretty, kindly, Jo-ann-y?" When she nodded excitedly, he continued.

"Wonderful. Now, put on your slippers and follow Witherwix. As with us by your side, Super Happy Fun Land is ever only a giggle away."

Joanna excitedly slipped on her pink Sugar Melon Watermelon Bop fluffy slippers.

The clown's stamper vanished in the blink of an eye as he offered her his hand, which now seemed much too big for his arm, like it was a cartoon. She placed her hand in his, and together, they stepped through the closet and into the world beyond. There was a sharp chill, a light, and spinning sparklers as her ticket burst into fireworks in her hand.

Joanna looked back for only a moment as her closet door creaked shut. The last she saw of her room were the sticky red footprints left by Witherwix's squeaky, oversized shoes.

SLAUGHTER AT SALLY'S

Harper Valley, New York, July 13th, 2015

Seventeen-year-old Abbigail Hobbs was late coming home from the annual summer carnival that was held at the Harper Valley fireman's field. It had been a long night. It was late. The moon was huge and high overhead, glowing a deep yellow, and she knew she was screwed.

Her now *very* ex-boyfriend Jakey Kline, the six-foot-two, perfect-chiseled-face and biceps-for-days star running back of her high school, was supposed to have dropped her off back at her mom's house on Fifth and Lake by ten-thirty. At the latest.

It was now approaching 3:30 a.m. It was the morning of the night after she had hugged her mom, Sally, and her little brother Andy outside the line to ride the spinning teacups. It was where she had met up with Jakey and his tall barrel-chested, vacant-eyed lineman buddies, Ruffis and Jerald. She liked to think of them as dumb and dumber. And their flighty, giggly girlfriends, both cheerleaders, because of course they were. Because who else would get all starry-eyed over two hundred and ninety pounds of dumber-than-bricks muscle guys with the combined emotional range of a doorknob?

Abbigail had promised her mother that she didn't have to worry. That had been a lie, but she hadn't known it at the time. So, it wasn't an intentional one.

If that counted for anything.

Which, of course, she doubted it did.

She'd felt so warm and safe with Jakey. He was so nice to her. He said such sweet things and promised her the world, and that he would be her knight in shining armor, her gentleman.

And he had been, right up until he and his gang had split ways after funnel cakes and sodas by the concessions row, at which point Jakey had developed more groping tentacles than an eldritch horror.

But Abbigail brushed it off, swatting, blushing, and giggling away his advances. She hoped he would get the message that she wasn't letting him run the bases into home plate on the first date. Which seemed to work just fine until he got her in his shiny red car's leather seats. He'd insisted that she owed him at least some road head after how much cash he'd blown on her at the carnival.

Abbigail had laughed at this. Jakey just didn't understand he had no claim to any part of her body, no matter how many stuffed elephants he'd won or the number of touchdowns he scored. Women weren't vending machines that you were nice to and spent money on until sex fell out.

But Jakey disagreed.

She had said *no* multiple times, uncomfortably laughing off his persistent advances. Even slapping him away.

Jakey didn't like that.

Not at all.

She cried and fought like hell.

He thought *that* was funny.

She told him she was going to tell.

He hadn't thought that was funny.

Not at all.

That had gotten Jakey pissed.

So, push came to shove, and a black eye and fat lip later for her troubles, there Abbigail was, being driven home in a squad car by Mom's best friend, Sheriff Jane Anne Wattson.

Abbigail sat in the back of Jane's cage, hands folded over a borrowed dark blue department windbreaker, which covered her torn tank top as she stared numbly out the window. Trying not to think about how the coat smelled like an old gym locker that hadn't been opened in a month or two.

"You sure you don't want to talk about it, hon?" Jane asked, her voice cutting over her police radio chatter as she glanced over her shoulder.

Abbigail shook her head. Her swollen lip throbbed. She was hot, despite the squad car blasting the air conditioner, and she wasn't in the mood to talk. Besides, she didn't have to say a thing.

Jane knew.

The woman's soft blue eyes had gone dark and stormy with just one look at Abbigail when she had pulled up alongside her as she was walking along the narrows.

"It'll help," Jane offered with a glance at her from the rear-view mirror that Abbigail felt on her more than heard. She shook her head again, and Jane sighed but didn't push. She just drove along in painfully awkward silence until they pulled up to the childhood home Mom had inherited when Grandpa had passed in 2010 from Leukemia.

"That's weird." Jane braked in front of the house and, with a flick of her hand, put the car into park along the driveway, eyeing the house with obvious trepidation. Her mom's beaten-up old brown Ford pickup, another inheritance from Grandpa, sat in the driveway next to her newer Volkswagen. The lights were on in the house, and the porch was brightly lit. Had her mom stayed up all night waiting for her? It was very possible and would force Abbigail to answer even more painfully uncomfortable questions. Likely, her mom Sally was sitting there on the living room sofa, sipping coffee from Dad's chipped cheese-yellow Green Bay Packer's mug. Wrapped up in her ratty old fluffy pinkish bathrobe with her feet folded under her. And the dreaded *no-nonsense* glare in her eyes as she waited for her daughter to stroll in, once again, with another stupid excuse for being out late.

Mom wasn't unreasonable.

But she was a pistol when angry.

Especially when she was over-caffeinated, tired, and worried.

Abbigail felt awful.

She had been thinking about it the whole way home, from when she'd been ditched on the roadside—*"like the whore you are,"* according to Jakey. To the long walk down the narrows. To the even longer ride in Jane's squad car. It all weighed on her.

Mom had a lot to deal with. She was sick, just like Grandpa had been. Hereditary bullshit, but her physician insisted they had caught it in time to assure her a long, happy life if she kept up with treatments. They would kick cancer's ass. She was frailer, paler, and stressed, but all in all, she was amazing, and Abbigail knew she had to be pissed and worried sick.

Jane opened the back door and offered a helping hand, which Abbigail ignored as she climbed out with a resigned, anxiety-filled sigh. She fought against her body's urge to hyperventilate as she stared at her family home.

"You're coming in with me, aren't you?" Abbigail asked, half-dreading, half-hoping, because Jane was a great mediator whenever she made the mistake of getting mixed up in arguments between Abbigail and her mom. Like the one time Abbigail had been caught shoplifting at the mall. It hadn't been her first time swiping shit from there, but it had been the last time. And for good reasons. She shuddered at the memory of Mom's ire.

Or the time she had gotten drunk off one of Grandpa's vodka bottles that she'd snuck into school, or the time she'd totaled Mom's old Kia right after getting her driver's permit. That had been bad.

This, however, was going to be worse.

Way worse.

Jane nodded. She didn't say a thing; she didn't have to, by the determined way she had her hands on her gun-belted hips as she stared from under the brim of her badged campaign hat, sighing long and hard. She was determined. Abbigail was honestly one part relieved that Jane was there, and the rest of the parts boiling with raw-ended anxious energy and anger.

She wanted to throw up.

She wanted a shower.

She wanted to scream.

She wanted to sleep.

Her belly was full of the bad kind of fluttering, nauseatingly flip-flopping butterflies, and they were making her nauseous, her heart race, and her head throbbing all at once.

"Okay," she managed.

"Is Sally starting to keep all the lights on?" Jane let out a long, low breath, shaking her head and pursing her lips with obvious trepidation "I know the chemo is kicking her ass, but I don't ever remember seeing the lights on this late. Something going on I should know about, hon? Is it getting…" She eyed Abbigail as they headed up to the porch.

"You've driven by often enough to see the lights not on this late?" Abbigail dismissively asked with an angst-raised silver-ringed brow.

"I've passed by." Jane shrugged. "Once or twice."

Abbigail narrowly eyed her. Jane had been her mom's best friend since kindergarten. Abbigail had also never seen or heard of her having a boyfriend, not even one. Not in her whole life. She was the closest thing to family outside of her mom and brother that Abbigail had left. So, she knew Jane better than most people. The woman wasn't open about it cause the town was still stuck in the fifties and got weird about such things, but Abbigail knew Jane was very (not-so-secretly) in love with Mom.

Probably always had been.

And her mom was clueless. Which had to be Hell for Jane, Abbigail mused while peering out the window. Trying to mentally prepare for her mom's knee-jerk reaction to her walking in the house well past curfew, *again*, and worse still, telling her about Jakey. *May as well get this over with*, Abbigail resolved with a sigh, breathing out a long string of emotion as Jane fumblingly pressed to recover from outing herself for stalking the house.

"I like to check in, you know," The Sheriff breathed helplessly. "Make sure things are… Kosher…"

"Creepy." Abbigail snorted as she pulled the blue *Sheriff's Department* windbreaker about her chest and headed to the house with a dreadful gnawing, clawing feeling hollowing out her heart and belly.

This was going to suck.

"You know," Jane seemed to struggle to find the words as she walked after her, "on patrol."

"Uh-huh," Abbigail scoffed.

"Oh, come on," Jane sighed. "I'm worried about my friend."

"Sure." Abbigail snorted.

Jane groaned but went silent as she escorted Abbigail up the cracked cement path bordered by a dandelion-infested lawn long overdue to be mowed. To Abbigail, each creaky stair of the warped steps to the house felt like her coffin door was closing her in, each beat of her pulse like the casket nails being harshly hammered into the wood. The times Abbigail had previously snuck out and ignored her curfew over the years burned white-hot in her memories. Regretfully relived, one by one, with gut-churning, vivid clarity. She'd concocted some wild excuses for those escapades. None of which had been believed or well-received.

So what were the odds of Mom believing her this time?

When she wasn't actually *trying* to worm her way out of a grounding?

It was unfair. Cause this time, it really wasn't her fault. However, unfortunately, stemming the tide of scolding her mom would likely heap on her the moment she stepped in the door long enough to tell her that. And then convincing her it wasn't a load of bullshit. Even the idea of *telling her…*

Her heart racing and a cold sweat of anxiety clammily slicking her forehead, Abbigail leaned on the peeling railing as she went. Then, after choking back a sob, she walked extra slowly to the door. She stood there for a long moment, hand on the tarnished brass knob, steeling herself, fighting the urge to run as fast as she could to the treehouse Grandpa had built. She wanted to hide up there forever. Her little fortress of solitude. She'd spent hours up there, reading comics and her mom's old Babysitters Club books whenever she needed space to think or an escape. And Abbigail had never needed to escape more than she did at that very moment.

"It's going to be okay," Jane lied.

"Right," Abbigail breathed. "Sure, it is."

That said, she opened the door.

And screamed.

She expected a lot of things. Perhaps Mom throwing Dad's mug at her as she came through the door. Maybe Mom staring silently in the *I'm going to murder you when Jane pushes off* kind of way she normally did whenever Jane showed up with her in the back of her squad car. Maybe even arguing until Abbigail ran to her room, slammed the door, then barfed herself into seeing stars from the whole Goddamned experience.

Anything but this.

Most of Sally lay sprawled on the couch. The rest of her was drying in clumps on the floor or mangled and dangling off the red-stained coffee table.

"*Andy!*" Abbigail screamed. Her little brother was the first and only thing she could think of. She sprinted past the horror show that had painted her family's living room red and down the hall, following huge sticky footprints on their white carpet. It was new, and Mom had always insisted that everyone take off their shoes when they came into the house. Abbigail had no idea why she thought of this, why that stuck, why that was even there in her head after what she'd just seen, but she couldn't shake it as she ran to her little brother's room. She reached it, her heart thundering in her chest as Jane tearfully screamed after her to stop and not go in.

Abbigail didn't care what Jane said. She stared at the Ninja Turtle poster held up by space shuttle puffy stickers and the Sesame Street sign spelling out ANDY and wrenched the door open. The doorknob was tacky with blood. Her mom's blood. It covered Abbigail's hands, warm and cloying. It smelled like hot, freshly poured iron as she pushed her way in. Praying, hoping, then once again—screaming.

Andy's room was empty.

She checked under the bed, in the closet, and all his other favorite spots to play *hide-and-go-piss-off, Abbigail.* Each one was still, spine shiveringly cold. No, Andy. She stood and picked up the one thing that was out of place: a large, shiny golden ticket. It gleamed like polished gold in the moonlight pouring in past Andy's star scape NASA curtains adorned with rockets and planets. She held it in her trembling, blood-caked hands and stared. It was inscribed with a stylized black logo of a creepy smiling clown in a pointy hat on one side and a circus, tents, and rides all on the other. A smiley face with her little brother's name all about it in a tidy, perfect circle, had been stamped into the foil.

Then, in the center of the ticket, in big, bold black letters, it said:

"Admittance paid in full for one to Super Happy Fun Land. Nontransferable, no refunds, no take-backsies. Once stamped, this ticket grants eternal admittance for the named ticket holder only."

SLAUGHTER-VERSARY

Abbigail stared at Mom's house through the side-view mirror of her truck. It was hot, and it was raining, droplets dribbling down the glass of her grandpa's hand-me-down truck that had passed from cancer to her mom, then from murder to Abbigail.

The bank had taken the Volkswagen, not that she cared. She couldn't bear to look at the spot where Andy's booster seat used to be, and finding the Cheerios and dried-up old gummies he'd dropped everywhere in the back seat was a nightmare. A knife reinserted and twisted in the barely scabbed-over wound that had plunged deeply into Abbigail's very soul when her family had been so brutally, senselessly ripped away.

The rain grew harder and harder as she sat there, hammering on the metal roof of her old truck and listening to Mom's favorite old Nirvana cassette tape, the Bleach album. *About a Girl* grungily rocking from the speakers. The music perfectly fit into her bleak mood, speaking grittily to her wounded heart. She watched the colorful realtor sign on a perfect white pole that had been hammered into the overgrown lawn, swaying creakingly in the deluge, proclaiming the property for sale. Somehow, seeing it made it all hurt all the more. Like picking at a fresh scab.

The dull, persistent ache of it was a nagging throb tugging biting tears from her eyes.

The house had been gutted, redone, and repainted, but she couldn't go in. As far as she was concerned, it was still covered in her mom's blood. That's all she could see when she went inside. Red, iron, stinking gore dripped down the fresh white paint and stained the fresh white Berber carpeting that had been installed to entice prospective buyers.

Jane had taken her in. She had done it all: the house, the renovation, organized the funeral. Jane had held onto her when she woke up crying and hugged her when she'd been so angry she didn't have the words to express it. She had been there through it all, through Abbigail's therapy. And pills. She had a shit ton of those, too. Jane had made sure she had what she needed.

Abbigail had considered saving them all up, hoarding them, and taking them all at once, punching her ticket out of the numb misery of life, because what the fuck did she have to live for?

But that feeling had died as a new determination set in. She wanted to know—no; she didn't *want* to know—she *needed* to know: why and who? Why had this happened, and who had done it? And yet, despite Jane being overjoyed to see life in Abbigail's eyes again, she refused to help her get that closure and understanding. Cutting Abbigail off from the one thing that would help her, details of the investigation into catching her mom's killer and her little brother's kidnapper.

It was infuriating. The one person she had in the world who could help her wouldn't.

In fact, Jane got angry and shut down every time Abbigail brought it up. Snapping at Abbigail whenever the question arose as to where things stood with the hunt for answers to what had happened on that terrible night. This had left Abbigail empty, yearning, bitterly prying into the case that now, frustratingly, was going nowhere. No arrests. No leads, no updates, nothing. Just ringing, empty silence.

There hadn't even been an Amber Alert for Andy. His picture wasn't on any milk cartons or in the news or papers. He was just gone, and the whole world seemed to be helping him vanish. No one would tell Abbigail why. Jane was stonewalling her. She was scared, Abbigail could tell, and no one else in town would talk about it, either. Insanely, everyone just acted like she was nuts for asking questions.

Because no one seemed to even remember she had a brother, and the ones that knew him…

That was worse.

They avoided her like she had the plague when she wouldn't stop looking, digging, and asking hard questions. It had gotten worse after she'd made fliers and spent an evening stapling them to telephone poles. She woke up the next morning, and they were all gone. Ripped down. Just torn corners of white paper stapled into the beams, lonelily flapping in the breeze where the *MISSING* poster with the picture of her brother had been just hours before. She'd tried posting about it on social media, but her account got suspended every time.

To add agony to insult her phone's cloud storage—all the pictures and videos, every single one? Gone. It was all gone. Evaporated without a trace into cyberspace.

It was like the whole world was aiding whoever had destroyed her family, chipping away at every remnant of them. Every shred of proof they had ever existed vanished bit by bit. Even the stuff from the house, the family photos from the walls, nearly all of it was gone, boxed up, locked away. "Evidence." She didn't have any hope she would ever see any of it again.

Jane had begged her to stop, and her psychiatrist and counselors had begged her, too. They all tried to psychobabble her into believing that forgetting was better and that she should concentrate on just letting go and starting fresh instead of obsessing over the case, but Abbigail wouldn't.

She wouldn't bring herself to let them go.

She wouldn't forget Andy.

Everyone else had.

She *couldn't.*

After posting the video of herself outside her family home where she talked about the murder of her mom and subsequent kidnapping of her brother, insisting it was all being covered up—

Well…

After that, the only one who'd approach Abbigail in a social setting with a ten-foot pole was Jane.

She was a pariah to everyone else; she was the town's crazy person. A psycho. A freak. People even went the other way in stores if they saw her in an aisle. It was awful. Her friends ghosted, people she grew up with treated her like a stranger, like she didn't even exist. It had left her numb. Broken.

But determined.

She existed in a holding pattern, going through the motions.

She'd graduated, barely.

She was eighteen, and she didn't care. Her mom had planned to take her camping for her eighteenth birthday. Sally had wanted to go on a family trip, hauling her grandpa's old Airstream that she had in storage with his old truck. It was her way of bringing him with them, as they hoped for campgrounds and parks for a summer of fun. Celebrating Abbigail's graduation and her first year of "official, legally recognized womanhood," and another year of her mom saying "fuck you" to cancer all at once. That had been the plan. Which had died with her family.

Abbigail had another plan, though.

From her pocket, she pulled out the strange gold ticket she'd found on Andy's bed. It was crumpled; she had stolen it out of the file in Jane's office at her house, which the sheriff desperately wanted her to think of as her own home, but Abbigail ended up feeling like it was more of a pity prison. One where she was locked down. Looked at with sad eyes and kept out of the loop on the murder kidnapping cases. She had seen the case file only twice.

And then Jane had learned to lock it up. There were lots of names in it, going back for years, with gaps in between. Documenting in faded, stained manila folders a horror she hadn't ever imagined was possible. It had been going on for ages, and no one talked about it. Frustratingly, whenever it was brought up, everyone acted like they had no idea what she was talking about.

Every ten years.

Another kid...*gone without a trace.*

Vanished off the face of the earth.

At least one of their parents were all brutally murdered—sometimes their whole families were annihilated along with them or soon after them. Some of the gruesome crime scene photos were black and white, and others were so old that they were yellowed with age. Every case had a ticket, just like Andy. But Andy's had been the only one in the box, in a clear, signed plastic evidence bag.

Who was doing it?

It made no sense, the gaps, the time. It couldn't be one person; no one lived that long.

So, was it some kind of sicko cult? Copycats?

She aimed to find out.

The most recent noteworthy name in the investigation was Fredrick Von Whipple, or, as he was known, "Freddy Whipple." In 2005, ten years to the day, at around three a.m., Freddy's wife Mary had been butchered, just like Abbigail's mom had been. And his daughter Joanna had vanished, just like Andy.

Freddy had almost died as well, but the file was thin on him, other than to state he'd been critically injured and too badly traumatized to add much to the case. But his file was the only one in the box that didn't have a red *DECEASED* stamped on the front. That made Freddy Whipple her last hope of finding any answers.

She called him. It hadn't taken much to find him, just a search online, and boom, there he was—up and relocated to San Francisco. Frustratingly, there was little else. She called. He hadn't answered.

So, she kept calling.

Leaving messages.

Day after day.

Until one day, he called back and agreed to a meeting.

A crappy-looking sedan pulled up, parked, and a man stepped out. He looked at the house, then her truck, like he was considering getting back into his car. Then he punched his thigh, pulled his jacket over his head a bit, and then scurried to Abbigail's passenger side door. He stared into the window at her.

He looked so old. His face was so lean and sickly that it looked like pale corpse skin stretched over a skull. His eyes were piercing, a dolefully dark brown that had no spark, no soul behind them as he glared at her before yanking open the door and getting in.

"Let it go," he growled before he'd even settled in the seat.

Abbigail said nothing at first, gazing past him into the rain at her old house as *Papercuts* played from her hand-me-down truck's cassette player.

Freddy eyed the cassette deck, then her, as if to ask "Seriously?" Each word was like a memory of her mom rocking out with her old Walkman while vacuuming. Or it loudly blaring out of the old silver boombox she'd kept in the kitchen while she cooked. Using the spatula or spoon in her hand as a make-believe microphone while she rocked out to her favorite band, cooking for her favorite people.

That's what her mom called them.

Andy and her.

Her favorite people.

That memory hit hard.

Like a mule kicking her to the gut.

Violently driving the air out of her lungs, Abbigail allowed the perfect, gritty song to grind out a few more verses, then irritably reached out and shut it off before eyeing the older man. It felt empty in her truck when the music abruptly ended. Lonely and achingly full of ghosts.

"Nice to meet you, Freddy." She gave a melancholic sigh, choking back tears as she sat back in her seat, resting her head on the headrest, and closed her eyes.

"Yeah, right." The older man snorted derisively as he glanced out the window at the house. Staring at it hauntedly. "This where it happened, then?"

Abbigail nodded.

"That sucks. Believe me, I know." He eyed her as he wiped the rain off his gaunt, faintly jaundiced face and shook his unkept hair. "But let it go. You have to, please, just let it go."

"I can't." Abbigail sharply breathed.

"Okay, look." Freddy groaned. "It's not an option. You *have* to, or it gets worse."

"Tell me, Freddy," Abbigail snapped. "My mom's dead, my little brother is gone, my family home is up for sale, everyone thinks I'm crazy. What do I have left to lose, to be afraid of? How can it possibly get worse? What the fuck do I have to live for, except this?"

"You have your life, kid," Freddy snapped back as he eyed her, his gaze withering, wide, and pleading all at once. "And trust me, you have a lot to fear and a lot more to lose, and it can get so much worse if you don't leave it be."

"You call this a life?" Abbigail snapped, then frowned, as the rest of what he said caught up with her. Leaking through her was a hot flaring of rage at him, dismissing her like a wet blanket tossed over a fire and then doused in a bucket of icy cold water.

He flinched and jabbed a trembling finger toward the crumpled, shiny ticket in her hand. "Get rid of it. Dear God, just get rid of it, burn it, bury it, put it back wherever you found it. Just let it go and never think about it again."

"It's all I've got left. I've gotta find my little brother. Or at least find out what happened to him and who did it and stop it from happening to any other families."

Freddy sharply breathed as he let his chin droop to his chest. "You've got no idea what you're doing. No idea what's coming if you do this. Why won't you listen?"

She stared at him. "I can't listen if no one's talking. You all know something I don't."

"Christ Almighty," Freddy groaned, scrubbing his hands over his tired face. "Trust me, kiddo," he rasped woodenly. "You don't want to know, and the reason you don't is that someone loves you enough to protect you from it. Just respect that."

"I can't…" Abbigail trailed off, watching a sheriff's department squad car slowly pull up. Jane got out. Her hat was encased in a wired plastic bath cap-like thing as she stepped out of her car, eyed the house, and shivered. Then she pulled her green jacket closed and headed to Abbigail's window with a determined gait. She rapped firmly on the glass.

Slowly, bitterly, Abbigail rolled it down and stared at the woman who wanted to step into her mom's shoes, but she couldn't. Her mom was buried in a box in the local boneyard.

"Thanks for calling, Freddy." Jane nodded at him with grim appreciation, and he nodded resignedly back.

"You called her?" Abbigail's head swiveled angrily about, and the man grimaced.

"You didn't give me a choice, kiddo." Freddy gruffly shrugged. "You saw the file, right?"

Slowly, Abbigail nodded.

"Ever wonder why I'm the only one in it that's still alive?"

Abbigail stared at him.

"We've got a lot to talk about," Jane grimly stated in a voice that brooked no argument. "Follow me to Mikey's, I'm buying. You, me, and Freddy, we're going to have us a long overdue conversation."

SLASHER AND A SLICE

The rumble of Skee-Ball and the riot of electronic noises flooding the dining area from the busy arcade at the back of the pizzeria plucked at Abbigail's last frayed nerve. With her head resting against her fist, her slice of New York style pie sat cooling on her paper plate alongside an untouched glass of root bear. She wasn't hungry; she rarely was these days.

Freddy and Jane sat in silence in the corner booth at the back of the local pie shop. The two kept eyeing each other between bites. Freddy looked pained and bitter. Jane was pale, frightened, but somehow reserved as they sipped at their straws and ate.

Not saying a word.

It all felt mechanical, like no one knew where or how to start. Abbigail's frustration and impatience mounted as she glanced out the window at the gray, rainy, miserable afternoon and waited for the time-wasting to end. And then, all at once, she couldn't take it anymore and got up.

"This is a waste of time."

Jane calmly lowered her half-eaten slice and sat back, eying Abbigail, where she stood in a way that was unnervingly stilling as she stared right back at her.

"Sit. Down." Jane pointed at the booth Abbigail had just vacated beside Freddy, loudly slurping Mountain Dew from his straw.

"You," Abbigail snapped, "are not my mom. I'm eighteen. I can do what I want. You can't fucking stop me. You just can't. So, *back off*."

"Yes," Jane snapped back, with a cold flash in her eyes that Abbigail had never seen before. "I can stop you. So sit down or I'll think up something to cuff you for and leave you to cool off in the precinct's fucking cage for the night, like the grown-ass woman you claim to be, young lady."

"You can't," Abbigail gasped. She stared with wide eyes of glassy shock at the woman who looked about as deadly serious as Abbigail had ever seen her. Jane glowered right back and didn't flinch. Not even a little.

"I think I can make a case for tampering with evidence. You do have that golden ticket in your pocket still, right?"

Abbigail froze. She had never hated Jane before, not until this very moment. Sure, she'd been frustrated by her. Irritated? Yeah, definitely. Angry? Yup, of course, how couldn't she have been?

But hate? No, never.

Not until just in that precise, painful moment.

Abbigail was shaking.

Why couldn't Jane understand? Why didn't she care how Abbigail felt?

How could Jane not see that she needed this, so, so, so, so, badly?

For a moment, once again, the only sound at the booth was the chaos from the arcade as an uncomfortable silence settled over the three of them. Then, with a hot flush rising on her neck and an uncomfortable tightness in her belly, Abbigail reluctantly sat. Hesitantly, she withdrew the golden ticket and placed it on the table between them. Both adults leaned away from it, like it was diseased, as she spoke. "Yeah. I have it. I have Andy's ticket. And I want to find who left it, and…and…"

"And what?" Freddy chuckled darkly. He wasn't making fun of her or mocking her. He sounded angry, but not at her, but like he was angry alongside her. And yet all these years, he'd done nothing himself, nothing but waste away and let the horror go on and on.

How did he live with that?

Then, as he gazed hollowly back at her with sunken, sleep-bagged, bloodshot eyes, she realized that Freddy *couldn't* live with it. He hated himself, and he felt like he was alone and helpless. He was breathing, but empty, gone. And as heartbreaking as that was, it didn't make sense.

"I can't be you; I can't do…nothing. I have to stop it…"

"How?" Freddy asked. He took a sip of his soda, slurping at it loudly while maintaining pointed, meaningful eye contact.

He then unexpectedly lifted his faded black Zach Wild *Wilden tour 1999* t-shirt, just up to his color bone. His hairy, sweaty skin was painfully pale, but what was paler were the horrific scars crisscrossing his chest and stomach. Some of them were an inch wide, others looked like thin claw marks that had bitten deep. It looked like he had been mauled by a fucking god-dammed lion.

"I was dead, kid." Freddy shivered out with a pained grimace. "Dead as a fucking doornail. Three times. The EMTs brought me back, then the hospital brought me back as they put my insides back inside me. Then I stroked out, and they brought me back again. I don't know if I can ever forgive them for that bullshit. Saving me. Supposed to be three strikes and you're out. That would have been a fucking mercy. What the fuck do I got to live for?"

Freddy crudely mimicked her earlier question with a snarl as he jabbed a finger at his scars. Particularly the bit that looked like something had sliced off a huge chunk of his belly skin, slice by slice.

"My life is pain." He looked like he was going to cry, or be sick, or maybe both. "That's what I got left. You got more than that. You've got it all, kid. You don't know how fucking lucky you are. You've got Jane, a chance to build something new, a future. Me, I get endless night terrors that make me buy rubber sheets for the crappy bed that I piss in every night and wake up alone and screaming in a crappy apartment, to live a crappy, fucking life."

Abbigail gaped, horror-struck, as he dropped his t-shirt, and it flumped back down over his gaunt, massacred torso. "I've seen shit you wouldn't believe, kiddo, enough to know to leave it be. There ain't shit you can do. So, don't. For the love of God, choose to live."

She sat there, stunned.

The ghost of Freddy's scars haunted her vision, hovering over everything as she tried to blink it out of her sight. It wasn't going anywhere; it wasn't something so easily forgotten. Yeah, Abbigail mused uneasily, that sight was going to live rent-free in her brain. Likely forever.

This was a lot to take in.

She had no idea.

It was dangerous; Abbigail had been painfully aware of that going in but had plowed on ahead, regardless. She had thought he'd help her, help her find meaning, find a way to make it stop. She had expected resistance, resistance that was something she could deal with, *but this*. She hadn't expected this.

Fear.

A gut-wrenching stab of it sent a chill through her. She had seen what had been done to her mom—and that was burned into her soul, the carnage, the gore, the horror of it. But this, somehow… this encounter drove that deeper. Seeing what'd happened to Freddy somehow drove that emotion home like a railroad spike hammered into her chest by a sledgehammer.

A painful reality she wasn't quite ready to accept.

Abbigail felt it coming.

Hot, stinging tears.

Anger, sadness, hopelessness, and frustration boiled and distilled into misery in tear form as they brimmed and then dribbled down her cheeks. This was just wrong.

All sorts of wrong.

And neither Jane nor Freddy seemed to be able or willing to do anything about it. She glared frostily at both, one at a time. Then she froze when she caught sight of the pained, tearful look on Jane's face as the woman wiped her eyes with her hand and took a long, ragged breath.

"This has been going on for years, honey. Years, and years and years, going back…no one knows how far." Jane shook her head and shuddered. "My file is just the most recent one. There are more, lots more, and not just here. We don't know how widespread it is 'cause not every agency wants to cooperate, and some don't even want to concede that it's real, but we think it's everywhere, and no one can stop it."

"Folks have tried." Freddy nodded. "We think that's the other reason the cases are so hush-hush; no one talks, and everyone who looks too hard into the golden ticket murders gets got. They vanish or get slaughtered. Then, in all cases, they just go ice-cold, get buried, get forgotten, and get swept under the rug. It's every ten years that it revisits a place on the anniversary of another kidnapping and killing. Moving around from town to town, place to place. Month by month. It spaces it out, gives people time to forget."

"And they do," Jane said. "I've got no idea why, but most people, they repress it or something—'cause after a few weeks, the ones who know about the cases, the ones who knew the victims…they forget."

"Most of the time," Freddy sighed, eying Abbigail like she was a stinky bug that had landed on his slice of pizza. "Then there's us." He took a bite, glared at her some more, then shook his head. "Some folks, like us, it sticks to our craw. We remember…we can't help it."

"And usually," Jane added, "The ones that can't let go, the ones who can't forget, they vanish. Or worse…"

"Yup."

"Some people call whoever, or whatever, is doing it *The Golden Ticket Slasher*," Jane spoke in a harshly secretive whisper, like she was afraid people might overhear her talking about it. "But there isn't much else we have on it. Just boxes and boxes of files full of names of missing children and dead families. And whoever the Golden Ticket Slasher is, well, they're like a ghost. No suspects, no motive, no rhyme or reason, just abductions and murders all over the map going back decades."

"You two are acting like the psycho doing all this is some kind of fucking boogie man." Abbigail scoffed; the pair were behaving like terrified kids. Sure, killers were scary. But Jane had a gun, knew how to use it.

Freddy, well…

He was half gone already.

One foot in the grave and the other itching to catch up.

Freddy laughed.

It was a low, sickly sound. "I don't know what The Golden Ticket Slasher is, but a boogeyman is as apt a description as any I've found." He exchanged looks with Jane. "I risk a lot saying even as much as I have already. Every other person who's flapped their gums…" He paused to cross himself nervously over the chest like he was warding off some kind of supernatural evil. "They vanish, and people forget them, too. That, or they just end up dead. *It* doesn't like snitches. I may have already said too much."

It was a lot of information. Abbigail tried to wrap her head around it. "Surely someone *has* talked about it, though, right? At some point?"

"None that lived long," Freddy repeated with a furtive look about like he expected the clown to be waiting over the shoulder with a knife poised to carve him up to pieces good and proper.

"And if you don't let it lie, Abbigail, it'll come for you next," Jane choked out in a sound close to a sob.

"It'll hunt you down," Franky added with brutal bluntness, "and you'll end up just like my Mary or your mom did. Or, if you're unlucky, like me." He pointed meaningfully at his chest. "Nowhere's safe."

"So that's why you moved…" Abbigail asserted, "to San Francisco."

"Yup. And I drink myself silly and keep my damned mouth shut. I moved on. 'Cause I saw what it did to my poor Mary. It fucking *butchered* her. It should have killed me too, but it didn't." He grimaced, an agonized amusement lit to his face as he chuckled. "Though not for lack of trying."

"You *saw* it," Abbigail gasped.

"Nope, sorry," Freddy breathed out in a long, fearful breath. "Don't even ask."

"Read it," Jane interrupted. "Flip it over and read the fine print along the edges."

Abbigail stared at the ticket Jane was pointing at, shining there on the table, and realized she'd never flipped it over. Just stared at its front, where her brother's name was punched into it around a smiley face. She picked it up, flipped it over. Sure enough, along the edges in print so fine that at first it seemed to be a solid black line were words in perfect seams along the golden ticket's edge.

She squinted.

It read:

"Super Happy Fun Land is an infernal trademark and as such is protected from infringement, impersonation, investigation, defamation, or conversation by any third parties. For any trademark questions, please refer to the Carnival Way for clarification. All rights reserved; all infringement punishable by clowning."

"What the fuck is *clowning*?" Abbigail asked. "It sounds like a gag joke gift. What does it mean?"

"It thinks it's funny." Freddy choked uncomfortably out as he eyed the ticket. "What it does to people…like it's some kind of sick joke."

"So, what?" Abbigail eyed him, feeling like a teakettle about to boil. "It's a guy dressed as a clown or something? That's who's doing this? What did you call it again? The Golden Ticket Slasher? *A fucking clown boogeyman of some kind?* Are you fucking serious right now?"

Freddy went paler than seemed possible at her words, flinching away like she'd slapped him.

"This is the most insane bullshit I've ever heard!" Abbigail snapped.

"Abbigail," Jane whispered, her jaw trembling as she spoke, sweating like she was in the hot seat of her precinct's interrogation room with the lights shining down particularly brightly on her.

"Please, you've gotta let it go. Please, baby. For your mom, for me… Can you do that for me, sweetie?"

"What about Andy?" Abbigail slammed her fist on the table so hard that her hand went numb. "What am I supposed to do, forget about my little brother and leave him in this creepy-ass Super Happy Fun Land?"

Jane went pale, but Freddy looked like he was going to be sick. "I've got to get out of here," he whispered. "Please let me go, please, I don't want to die…"

SNITCHES GET SMASHED

Harper Valley, New York, July 13th, 2016

Freddy got into his car and started driving. He could barely breathe, and he could barely see straight, but he had to get away. Away from *her*. The windshield wipers squealed and his hands white-knuckled at the leather-covered steering wheel. He kept glancing up to the aged strip of silly photos he'd taken with his daughter at the carnival the day before she'd vanished and his wife had been murdered. It was a long rectangle of happy memories: sticking out her tongue and making antlers with her hands over her head, and him making his own awful, goofy face that had always made her laugh.

There were six of those tiny memories, laughs captured in fading laminated paper, which were the last remnants that proved he'd once been a dad to a wonderful little girl who'd been his whole world and heart. And he couldn't even bury her. He couldn't even admit she had existed. She was just gone.

Tears, hot and itchy, trickled down his cheeks. The world was a wet haze, painted in shades of blue and gray, starred by blurred lights and buildings that were just obscure shapes behind a veil of gloom as his car sped out of Harper Valley. He passed other drivers, he ignored the speed limit, and he even ran a few red lights on his way out of town. He saw them—a dull pair of star-crossed blurs of red swaying in the torrential storm, hanging overhead. But he blew past them and kept going.

He passed the fireman's field and saw the carnival, and the pain came rushing in. His chest quivered with the sobs forced out of him, slapping the wheel repeatedly as the awful thing loomed large in the field. Silhouettes of rides, tents, and booths for games were all exactly as it was that one terrible day eleven years ago.

Joanna had loved the funhouse with the silly mirrors and scary props. She had loved the arcade with all the beeping and noise and the chink-chink of coins. The dull rumble and wooden *THUNK* of Skee-balls rolling and jumping into targets and the buzzing of dispensing tickets. His sweet little girl had adored the big wheel and treats. It had been a perfect day, except for that bit about the clown in the field…

The field.

There it was, just ahead. And standing in it, a figure in the deluge, a shadow still and dark amid the sheeting grays of the rain. Freddy's blood ran cold as he sped past, looking up to see its reflection in the rearview, poised there staring back at him with cat's eyes as it held a bunch of black balloons whipping and careening about in the wind.

Freddy sped up.

He had to get away.

Far, far away.

The rain hammered his windshield so hard that the wipers couldn't keep up. All he could make out was the blur of what he hoped was the road, but he couldn't stop.

He also didn't see the deer in time.

The animal bounced off Freddy's bumper and landed with a sharp shattering of glass and the crumpling metal of his hood. It rolled over the top and off the back of the car as Freddy yelled and slammed on the brakes. The horn blared as his car spun about, tilting and flipping along the side of the road until it came to a violent stop against the trees with a groan of ruined framework and a crushing, grating creak.

This is it, he thought with a despairing groan.

Then…

Pain.

Darkness.

He blinked. Blood and rain soaked his face as he hung upside down by the seatbelt he hadn't even remembered putting on. It'd probably saved his life, but now all the blood had rushed to his head and the belt dug into his skin, cutting off circulation. He struggled, flailing, fumbling with wet plastic, and at last released the buckle and fell hard. He landed with a grunt and crunch of glass and a stuttering gasp of air being driven out of his lungs onto a mix of smashed glass, old wet leaves, broken sticks and shrubbery, and thick grass.

He breathed hard, wincing at the pain. Everything hurt and his heart was thundering in his chest like a madman was hammering away at a big bass drum with two sticks. He eyed his daughter's picture. The one he kept in the elastic band over his driver's seat sun visor and grabbed it. "My guardian angel," he groggily murmured as he kissed it before squeezing painfully out of what was left of the shattered windshield.

He was alive. Nothing seemed broken. His mind was a blur of fear and adrenaline as he looked about in the downpour, raindrops popping up chest high in icy ricochets off the ground where it slapped loudly into the puddles and mud.

Overhead, the dark clouds boiled as dusk settled darkly over the rise of a full moon that peaked out of the lightning-splayed heavens. Beneath that moonlight, he saw it, a shape across the road holding a floating bunch of shiny black balloons. Its other arm was raised, urgently pointing a white-gloved finger at something on his side of the road. Freddy followed its direction and stared at a shape on the ground.

The deer?

Was it still alive?

How in the hell…

It got up, shook itself, and ran off.

But no, Freddy realized, it couldn't have been pointing at the deer.

Then what had it been pointing at?

Something behind him?

Freddy's blood froze as his pain and adrenaline-addled mind caught up to what he had seen, and slowly, tremblingly, sobbingly, he looked up again to the thing holding the balloons.

The clown. Still pointing, right past him.

"No," Freddy gasped. "I didn't tell…"

It didn't move.

It kept pointing.

"Fuck's sake, what do you want?" he screamed. "I moved away, I kept quiet, I didn't say a word except to tell her to stop! Please… please, no…" When the clown remained still, Freddy whimpered. "Do I have to look?"

And at last, it moved, if only to nod once with a jingle of bells from its floppy, pointed hat.

"Oh, God…" Frank shivered as he slowly turned around.

It was there, right behind him, its ghoulish white face and cat eyes glowing as it slammed a circus mallet into the side of his head and made everything go dark. The last thing Freddy heard were his own cries and the crunching squelch of his skull smashing like a ripe melon.

The clown stood over the mangled corpse, observing as the last of Feddy's twitches and life faded away. The body went still, a strip of pictures of him and his daughter Joanna in his hand, lying there in the crimson-stained puddles and mud.

Slowly, the smiling images on the strip of novelty booth photos depicting a perfect day at the carnival faded away to nothing. Bit by bit, the color bled into the water, leaving an oily, scummy film co-mingling on its surface as Joanna vanished completely. Followed soon after, by Freddy. Witherwix pointed down at the still-twitching corpse and cackled, clownish insanity ringing out over the trees. Scattering crows from the branches as his bunch of balloons floated away, high overhead, into the storm.

Naughty, Naughty Boy

Harper Valley, New York, July 13th, 2016

Jakey Kline watched from the arcade while his ex—the one that got away easy—left her booth, leaving Sherriff Cunt there, and trudged towards the door of the pizzeria with her arms folded over her spectacular tits. She looked crestfallen, cored out, and sexy as fucking hell.

He'd noticed them there almost immediately as he stuffed a five into the arcade's token exchange machine. He kept glancing over, looking between the gathering in the back booth and the zombie aliens he was killing with his blue plastic gun. Blasts, beeping, and screeches blared from the screen as he wiped out stage after stage with streak after streak. It was his favorite game, Area 51.

Just as Abbigail stood up, a little after the boomer dude had run off looking like he'd pissed himself, one of the aliens ate his last quarter of gameplay. He'd gotten distracted staring at Abbigail's ass.

She has a nice ass. Jakey smirked as he shot his initials into the top score screen, then holstered his gun back onto the game cabinet and watched her. Leaning there on the cabinet, taking her in from afar. The pizzeria's arcade was busy that night, with loads of kids playing Skee-ball and Ninja Turtles while teenagers duked it out on the shooters and fighting games, so she never saw him there. Something about being able to observe her unnoticed made him feel powerful. Excited.

Jakey had no idea what they'd been talking about, or what his ungrateful, psycho, prudish bitch of an ex was so upset about, but it made him laugh. He liked it when she cried. It got him a raging hard-on. She was just that way, sexy when she was all teary and bent out of shape.

He considered letting her go and snagging a grab-and-go slice and soda from the counter. Then he remembered that night in the car when she'd turned him down. He'd spent close to two hundred bucks at the carnival that night trying to buy his way into her tight, sweet, juicy ass, and she'd had the gall to say no?

She had, of course, told the sheriff.

Who had, of course, gone to his dad.

Who had, of course, made it disappear.

Who the fuck did the bitch think she was?

Didn't she know who *he* was, how many girls would give their left tit to have him? Even now, girls were lining up to get a ride before he left for Penn State on a sweet gravy train of a full-ride football scholarship… They all knew he was gonna be a star. An even bigger one than he already was. He was so good, so fast, that the ink was likely already drying on the Cowboys contract they were drafting to offer him a primo rookie spot on the team after he hit the field. His recruiter had told him as much. He was an NFL top draft pick, a pro team coach's wet dream of an up-and-coming collegiate all-star pigskin prospect.

Jakey had the look.

Jakey had the stuff.

Jakey was the big brand baller.

All Jakey needed was a few fly seasons of college ball and he was in like Flynn, balling with Bugatti's and bitches. Super Bowl rings and shiny things. That *was Jakey's future*. He smiled. He could taste the champagne bubbles and caviar dream street that he was on already. He'd have sponsors too, like maybe the Gillette ones. Those commercials always made him laugh. Maybe Nike? All the big stars had Nike commercials. And no one was going to be a bigger star than him.

Jakey Fucking Kline.

He was gonna be more loaded than his dad. Richy-rich, rich. A gold mine that could buy as much pussy as he wanted, when he wanted, whoever he wanted.

He glared at Abbigail.

The fucking bitch didn't get it.

She didn't understand how lucky she was to be wanted by Jakey *Fucking* Kline.

Should he go after her? Jakey eyed the outside world, past the flashing lights and dark of the arcade, through Mikey's pizzeria's glass storefront windows. It was raining hard.

Maybe he'd give her another chance. He was a nice guy; he could overlook that night's transgressions. She'd say yes this time.

Jakey smiled.

And even if she didn't, no one would believe her. Since her mom had died, she had gone bat-shit crazy. Everyone knew that. But crazy pussy was good pussy. Jakey considered his options a moment more as he watched Abbigail step out into the rain. Should he go and grab a bite and gulp, he wondered. He did love that pizza, and those cup-o-char pepperonis were killer. And he *was* hungry…

Then he laughed.

Nah.

Pussy, *then* pizza.

That was the bro code.

STAND YOUR GROUND

Harper Valley, New York, July 13th, 2016

All the walls had closed in as Abbigail listened to the story Freddy and Jane had told her. Shivering, she pulled her jacket about her as she fished her keys out of her pocket and started towards her truck. She paused by the alley in between the pizzeria and the town's comic book and joke shop and leaned against the wall, waiting for the nausea to pass. Sucking in icy breath after icy breath, trying to get her racing heart rate to tone it down before the wildly pumping organ blew up in her chest.

The Golden Ticket Slasher?

Jesus.

Her mind spun as she struggled to process it all, and…

Did she smell…peanuts? Roasting peanuts, popcorn… Cotton candy?

Why did it smell like a carnival had puked in the alley?

Abbigail pulled the ticket out of her pocket. "I'm sorry, Andy," she whispered. "I wish I could see you again and tell you that—Oh, Andy, I'm so fucking sorry…"

"Hey, bitch."

Abbigail jumped as Jakey Kline stepped into view. The back door by the arcade was leaking light and noise out into the trash-strewn alley as he invaded her personal space. "What'cha got there?"

He grabbed for the ticket, but she pulled away, recoiling as disgust and anger boiled within her.

"Get away from me!" she shrieked, scrambling to put some distance between them. Jakey laughed and strolled after her. He was sneering, that smarmy, overconfident, perfectly white and straight, ten-thousand-dollar dental work smile.

"Come on, baby," Jakey crooned. "You tried to end my football career, tried to get me cuffed and canceled… Couldn't keep your mouth shut, huh? I got something for you here." He grabbed at the crotch of his jeans and gave it a lewd squeeze as he humped the air, pointing it at her. "You won't be able to say much with your pretty little mouth full of Jakey cock, *huh*, snitch-bitch?"

Wide-eyed with horror and anger, Abbigail backed away, and he just kept advancing.

"Come on, you crazy, beautiful, fucking prudish bitch," Jakey purred. "I'm a forgiving guy. Give Jakey a proper bang for his buck and we'll call it even." He donned that same sickeningly charming smile he'd had that night in his car. The night he drove her out to Lover's Lane instead of bringing her home like he'd promised to after their date at the carnival. Where he'd…he'd—Abbigail's stomach lurched; she couldn't think about it. Just the sight of him was enough to make her nauseous, but thinking about *that*… Her skin crawled and her throat closed off like Jakey's hand was already wrapped around it.

No. Not again.

Not ever again.

"Stop playing hard to get," Jakey throatily warned as he advanced, his hand still squeezing lewdly at the crotch of his trousers. "Jakey just wants to play with you, good and hard."

No. Abbigail fumed. *Absolutely fucking not.*

Fear had all but smothered her into silence.

She fought it, though. Tooth and nail.

Finally, after choking back the mind-numbing horror grasping at her neck, Abbigail found her voice.

"Jakey." She snapped out the switchblade from her jeans pocket—a gift from Jane after that night. With a trembling finger, she pressed her thumb onto the trigger nub on its faux horn handle. The blade *snicked* smoothly out with a startlingly loud click that stopped Jakey dead in his tracks. *"Back the fuck off."*

Jakey's eyes went wide, first in confusion, and then in surprise.

"You try to touch me again, and I'll cut that poor excuse for a dick off of you, got it?" Abbigail hissed, her heart hammering dizzyingly in her chest as she thrust the small knife out before her.

He glared murderously, nostrils flaring, blue and yellow team jacket dripping. Neither of them said a word. Face flushed, water dribbling from her chin and bright blond hair, Abbigail didn't dare blink. She knew, with mind-spinning horror all the while, that Jakey, huge and terrifying there looming over her, could just grab her hand and take the knife away, then drag her into the alley before she could do a thing about it.

They stared one another down. A stalemate.

He *could have*, but he didn't try.

Big old Jakey, too scared to even make an attempt.

Jakey blinked first, backing away, seething. "My Dad'll hear about this," he hissed as he, step by step, retreated without once breaking eye contact. "Fucking psycho bitch."

Abbigail just stared at him as he crept like a worm back into the filthy hole he had emerged from. She felt sorry for the girls in his college. She was genuinely afraid for them. Jakey was a frat house nightmare packaged in a pretty silver-tongued box. The worst of the worst arrogant, rich, rapey, drunken college dude stereotypes imaginable, all in one, shoehorned into a high school letterman jacket.

But tonight, *this* girl had won.

Let's Play a Game

Harper Valley, New York, July 13th, 2016

Jakey watched Abbigail go from behind the pizzeria dumpster that smelled like a five-day-old August heated sauce and salad. He was seething, and he had to piss. But he couldn't look away—he hated that bitch, and he wanted to fuck her so badly. Abbigail stuffed her weird gold ticket into her pocket and sprinted to her shitty brown beater of a truck. She drove off with a squeal of near-bald tires, leaving a smog of exhaust behind.

"Bitch," he growled as he unzipped, whipped it out, and braced his free hand against the wall as he pissed on it. Grumbling under his breath, he sniffed and caught a stench of something off along on a chilly breeze that blew down the alley.

It was like a whiff of *wrongness*…

Jakey sniffed again, his nose wrinkling. "What the fuck?" he muttered, casting a look around. It smelled like a…like a carnival. Like hotdogs, cotton candy sweetness, and popcorn all at once, nauseatingly mixing with the sharp ammonia reek of piss and the putrid stench of steaming sunbaked garbage.

Then…

It was all at once unseasonably cold. Very, very cold. His skin puckered in fields of gooseflesh, and the hairs rising on his heavily muscled arms under his jacket as he sighed, shook it off, put it away, and zipped up his pants. Now he was outright shivering while seething as he stared at the road Abbigail had driven off on. "Bitch pulled a knife on me," he raged out loud, kicking over a trash can. "Me, *me* of all people? I am Jakey *Fucking* Kline."

"We know who you are, Ja-key." A nasal, giggly voice rumbled from the shadows. It wasn't like a normal voice; it echoed with ghosts of laughter and soft circus music. And it made his knees turn to Jell-o as he whirled about just as a shadow detached itself from the alley's dark walls.

"We'll play with you, Ja-key, *good and hard.*"

"What the fuck?" Jakey gasped, backing away as the circus freak from Hell advanced from the shadows with its weird-o Halloween mask of a face beaming. "What the fuck are you?"

It growled.

Like an animal.

The low, primal sound it emitted gripped at Jakey's insides and twisted them in an icy, clawed fist of iron terror. It smiled. A huge, red, wolfish smile at him that revealed rows of sharp yellow teeth.

"We are Witherwix the clown," it introduced while bowing with a sinisterly snickering, theatrical flourish. "Friend to good girls and boys, and their guide to Super Happy Fun Land." It paused and *tsked*, shaking a white-gloved finger at Jakey in disapproval.

"But you, Ja-key…Ja-key." It paused to indulge in a laugh that wasn't funny at all. "You, Ja-key, are a naughty, naughty boy. And we're afraid naughty, naughty boys and girls don't get to go to Super Happy Fun Land."

Jakey stared as the clown's smile faltered, the jovial glee melting away while shadows crept in from the lines of its sharply angular, grease-panted face. From within its black circled sunken sockets, its glowing, greenish-yellow cat's eyes widened to an impossible size.

"Oh no, we're afraid…" It mimed wiping at fake tears while it danced about and honked its squeaky nose. "…Boys like you, Ja-key. We carve out their dull brightness, and then, then they get to go to *the bad place*. It's the wicked woods for you, Ja-key. Yes, yes, indeed. Just the place to plant you." Its mirthless, predatory smile broadened. "There, you will shade the pretty snow and become a tree that howls forever at the big, bright moon."

This couldn't be real.

Jakey backed off even as it spun, tumbled, stepped, laughed, squeaked, and honked its way forward. One moment it was bounding off the brick wall in a flip, and in the next, it had him by the throat.

"Don't play *hard to get*, Ja-key," it snarled as it pinned him to the wall with one arm. Like he was nothing, light as a feather. It laughed liked Jakey was the funniest thing in the world.

"Are you ready for a game? The real fun is about to begin. Yes, we will play with you; oh, it will be such fun. We love this game, Ja-key."

Jakey gagged, the smell of carnival treats, piss, and trash nauseating his vision into swimming while he futilely struggled against the clown's iron-tight grip, slapping and punching to no effect while it pinned him there against the red bricks and squeezed until his eyes bugged.

"Do you like it, Ja-key?" Witherwix asked while it leered up at him in a way that had his bladder emptying again. Even though he had just pissed, he felt it, warm and wet, trickling down his legs. "Is it not such fun?" the clown giggled as Jakey gagged and whimpered.

Stuck there like a bug with a pin through it, fighting, wiggling, wobbling, and gurgling, but unable to remove the pin. The world was dimming.

All Jakey managed in the way of an answer was, *"Gawk, gawk…"* then a bubbly string of desperate, rasping gurgles. It drew a knife, big and silver, from its silk-cuffed, frilly sleeve. "We shall just keep going. Doesn't that sound like such fun? You know you'll like it. Isn't that right, Ja-Key? Isn't that what you say to all the nice girls who don't want to play with you?"

Jakey's terrified reflection gaped back at him in the blade's steel. Tears, hot and burning, welled up and streaked down his face. His coach's voice rang in his head, a loud baritone bellowing, and sharp screeches of the whistle rang out in his ears as he dangled there. *"There's no crying in football, no bitches get the ball! No balls, no ball, got it, boys?!"*

"Aww," Witherwix assured with a sick, twisted, gleeful nod. "It's a-okay, Ja-key."

The clown's glowing green eyes widened. It licked its blood-red lips with a black forked tongue like it was enjoying the game even more now that he was crying. Like it found his terror and pain to be delicious and mouthwatering.

"Please—" Jakey gasped. He sucked in air, no longer being choked, then he realized the clown *wanted* him to beg. He moaned through a thick heave of sobs. "Oh, God… Help me."

"God's not here, Ja-key," Witherwix purred as it caressed his face with the sharp end of its knife. "We already told you; it's the wicked woods for you."

It laughed, cold, high, and shrill. A peal of wild insanity warped as a blend of so many voices all at once.

Then the real pain started as silvery flashes rained down in stabs and slashes of hot agony, and Jakey screamed. Ja-key's terror and agony were drowned out by the laughter and cheering of gamers and the beeping, booming, and blasting sounds of the arcade blaring out of the open door into the pizzeria's arcade. In the back of his mind, he registered that no one could hear him. No one could help him. They would find his body later, tossed in the trash, and that was all that would remain of Jakey *Fucking* Kline.

CARNIVAL WAY

Harper Valley, New York, July 14th, 2016 – 1:00 a.m.

Abbigail leaned against her mom's red granite headstone in the Harper Valley Oaks cemetery and stared at her phone. She had surprisingly good internet reception in the town's meticulously landscaped boneyard. And so, ringed in by spikey iron fences and neat rows of dead people, this was her secret spot, her place to sit and talk or to just be with her mom. She felt close to her here, and as the moon hung watchful and full overhead, she searched and searched.

It felt like it had when she was little. Researching a paper on states, beavers, or bluejays for elementary school projects on her mom's heavy old Dell laptop. Mom had always been there with her, providing moral support as her tiny fingers hunted and pecked out words into the search bar.

"*I need to do it myself, Mommy,*" she'd always insisted, and her mom, Sally, had always grudgingly agreed. She sat and observed, sipping coffee or wine, as her daughter browsed and researched.

That memory hit Abbigail hard, like a mule kick to the gut. She hadn't meant that she wanted to do *everything* by herself, she thought angrily as her thumbs punched in letters and scrolled on her glowingly bright smartphone screen. She hadn't wanted to be alone.

Bitterness seeped up Abbigail's belly and throat like a geyser of bile, hot and nippy, as her mind wandered to all the times her mom had annoyed her. Times when she'd told her mom that she wished she was dead or hated her. Or how she couldn't wait to be grown and be able to do what she wanted.

She'd gotten her wish.

She hadn't wanted it.

Not really.

But somehow, that's what happened.

Then her mind wandered to Andy, and how she had gotten annoyed with him asking to play games when she wanted to doom scroll, text, read her magazines, or go out with her friends.

She lowered her phone to her lap and stared up at the moon. She'd have given anything to play with him again. Even if it was that stupid Battleship game he had loved, even if she had to watch a million repeat episodes of Blue's Clues and eat a whole pound of green jellybeans.

Anything.

She would do anything.

She had been searching for things about the tickets, picture searches, posts, scrolling endless chats and blogs and boards. Nothing. Plenty of creepy crap and gross porn, but nothing about the golden ticket slasher or murders. Zero results. Which, given what Jane and Freddy had told her, wasn't particularly surprising. But still frustrating. How could something so horrific just be allowed to go on and on and covered up and denied? Then a thought hit her like a lightning bolt as she considered the ticket. She typed in:

Carnival Way

Then stared at it where it sat in the search bar next to the blinking cursor, then, with a sigh of hope, hit *search* with her thumb and waited. In seconds, an actual result popped up.

Just one.

She clicked on the link.

Her eyes widened. Carnival Way was an actual location just a few hours away. It looked crappy. A blink-and-you'll-miss-it sort of place. The kind of place that most people with common sense would avoid. The town boasted little more than a string of shabby houses, a few brick buildings, a run-down library, a big storage facility, a trailer park, a tiny grocery store, a diner, and a single gas station. Somewhere, an empty plot of land for sale.

It was creepy.

The more she read, the more it both made sense and the more she didn't like it. It was an old town. Very old. Founded in the late eighteen hundreds by retired entertainers. Not like movie stars or famous comedians. Nope, jugglers, knife throwers, psychics, bearded ladies, animal tamers, carneys, and, yes, clowns. The freaks of society, that had no welcome to be found in normal towns. So they founded their own.

There were dozens of pictures of them all at the annual Carnival Way fest where hundreds swept into the huge fields to celebrate. Old clowns, young clowns. People learning to be clowns, mullet-sporting ride mechanics and game hawkers in blue jeans drinking cheap bear, men in tuxes and top hats, women in sparkly singlets. It was dizzying.

She scrolled through the webpage, clicking on photos and absorbing the information. The town even had a museum with an actual, honest-to-goodness clown historian in residence. She had no idea that was even a thing...

The more she read, the more she wanted to go, and the more she wanted to go, the more her mind screamed at her not to. Which, of course, only made her want to go there even more. But no matter how deep she delved, she didn't find anything creepier than a clown dating board that advertised that:

"Clowns don't have to be lonely at carnies only, page of carnal, carnival love. Satisfaction guaranteed."

Abbigail shuddered.

Gross.

She moved past it with an eye roll as a user named Happy-cream-pies-the-clown's post about wanting to find his clown queen made her want to puke.

Moving on.

Desperate.

Searching but not finding a thing.

So, she went back to the historian bit in the museum to grab the address. She snapped a photo of the golden ticket, back and front, and attached it to an email explaining what had happened. Begging Bozo the Know-It-All to help her. She crammed all her hopes into that one email. To a clown. She hoped this new, last-ditch effort wasn't as disappointing as Freddy had been.

Emotionally spent, Abbigail sat there a moment, watching the fireflies buzz whimsically about the gravestones in the moonlight. Give the time of night, she wasn't expecting a quick answer. So she went back to look up Freddy again. Trying to find out anything about him that would explain how a grown-ass-man could just let go after his wife was murdered and his kid was abducted by a clown.

A local result froze her in her tracks as a notification beeped to announce it on her phone.

It was in the *Harper Valley Crier*, the town's once newspaper, and now it's frivolously sleazy, modern online news outlet and gossip corner.

Her hands shook as she read it.

"Former Resident Fredrick-'Freddy' Von Whipple, 55, died today in a suspected DWI incident along the narrows."

There were photos.

The mangled car. The body covered by a tarp, only the feet showing among the wreckage.

It was awful.

But no one seemed to care.

Not a single comment, sad face or like.

Nothing for Freddy.

Then, more news.

Just in:

"DEAD: Town hero Jakey Kline, eighteen, son of Mayor Erik Kline and the playboy running back, shining star of the Harper Valley Saints who led the team to a second state championship victory in his senior year. Dreams of collegiate football glory shattered. A presumed family congenial heart condition blamed for an all-star elite athlete's death. More to follow."

The article already had hundreds of sad faces. Even as she watched, more comments with condolences poured in.

As she read on, a commotion of sirens and flashing lights drew her stunned attention up from her phone to the sight of Jane's patrol car. Full blues and reds lit up the night as the squad car screeched to a stop outside the boneyard's gate. She leapt out, screaming Abbigail's name.

HEART TO HEART

Harper Valley, New York, July 14th, 2016 – 6:00 a.m.

Jane had bags under her eyes, and she looked painfully thin as she rested her forehead in her hand and stared at her department laptop reading about Carnival Way.

"No." she shook her head and pushed the laptop away. "Number one, this whole town is a giant waving neon red flag. Number two: Let. It. Go."

"I can't—"

"*You have to.*" Jane cut her off with a thump of her fist on her desk that shook the pencils stacked like a pointy graphite and wooden bouquet in her 'World's Best Friend' mug that Abbigail's mom had given her last Christmas. Jane glared. "You don't get it, honey, do you?"

"Get what?" Abbigail snapped back.

"Freddy, Jakey, they're both dead. Likely offed by The Golden Ticket Slasher." Jane yanked out her phone, unlocked the screen, then pulled up a photo that Abbigail couldn't unsee.

It was what was left of Jakey.

He looked like he'd been crammed into a giant pencil sharpener and ground down to meat and bone. There was hardly an inch that wasn't stabbed or slashed to ribbons. He was barely recognizable, but it was him, lying there on a metal table in the shredded remnants of his letterman jacket.

She dry-heaved.

Hard.

Over and over.

She just made it in time to Jane's trash can to let loose a hot, gooey, chunky blast.

Jane watched it dispassionately, and as Abbigail finished wiping her mouth, she continued.

"Does this look like a congenital heart condition death to you, honey? This doesn't happen in our town, not but once every ten years, and this is outside of the pattern. No missing kid, no family ripped to pieces, just a slimy jerk of a teenager and Freddy."

Abbigail gagged again, but she had nothing left to barf up, and it just hurt and stung as the bitter nasty remnants in her throat burned hot. She swallowed hard, keeping her eyes averted as she sank back into her chair.

"Why would it go after…"

"I don't know," Jane admitted as she brought up a picture of the accident with a flip of her pointer finger on her phone screen and showed that to her next. "And I've never seen an accident like this."

Abbigail didn't want to look, but she couldn't help herself, and once she did, she couldn't look away. What she could only assume was Freddy was broken in ways she didn't think people could be broken: he was pulped. His head was a brutal mass of red, gray, and sharp white bits of cracked bone poking out of it. An eyeball stared from a string of nerves as it dangled from the mutilated heap.

Seeing all this made it too real, and memories of the carnage, the charnel house that the killer she now knew to be called the Golden Ticket Slasher had made of her home with her mom, butchering her too...

It was like a scab had just been ripped off a cut, raw and nipping and awful.

"He got out of the car," Jane whispered. "I know he did. Somehow, he survived that accident, and something did this to him afterward. We've got his footprints leading from the car wreck,"— She slid the screen up and displayed the deep muddy prints in the swampy grass—"and I don't know of any animal that does this to people, do you?"

Mutely, Abbigail shook her head.

"It's only been a year, and this thing's back because you won't stop. You have to let it go, honey. Your life, and a lot of other people's lives, depends on it."

"So." Tears filled her eyes and her heart hardened with anger. "This is my fault? Is that what you are saying?"

"Honey..."

"No," Abbigail said. "This is not my fault, no, no, no—"

"It's not about fault, honey." Jane snapped loudly enough to shut Abbigail down before it got enough steam to plow her over. "You didn't know. I tried everything but telling you, for obvious reasons, to help you through this, so you could live... Your mom would have wanted that for you."

"Don't tell me what Mom would want," Abbigail countered with a sob. "She wouldn't have wanted me to give up on Andy! She wouldn't, not ever."

Jane sighed with a defeated shake of her head. "She was my best friend, my everything." Jane looked like she was in agony as she spoke in a trembling emotional rasp, "She made me promise to look out for you when she first got her diagnosis; she even made me your guardian in case…" She winced as she sat there searching for words to continue, then, after a deep breath, went on. "So yes, I am going to tell you what your mom wanted. She wanted you to be happy. Andy is gone, and so is Sally, and I don't want you to go, too."

Abbigail stared. Sniffing, her chest heaving as she sucked in breaths and tried to be angry but couldn't.

"Your mom knew about this. It happened to us, too," Jane continued. "One of our friends when we were kids. Timmy Ward. His mom's house had cop cars one day, yellow tape, and then we saw the body bag rolled out from the house. Just one, his mom. We were kids, too young to understand and too scared to do any different, so we did what our parents said, and never spoke of it again."

She paused and glanced out the window.

"Freddy was older, but he knew Timmy as well. And everyone, especially the boys, knew his mom. She was the high school nurse. All the guys drooled over her. And then, no one spoke of her or her son again. We were told she had a heart-attack and that Timmy went away, but we couldn't say anything, or we could go away like Timmy and his mom."

It was unbelievable.

Before she could respond, her phone dinged. It was an email. From Bozo the Know-It-All.

Tomorrow. 3 p.m. Sharpish.

"What was that?" Jane uneasily asked.

"I emailed the clown historian in Carnival Way about the Golden Ticket Slasher, and he just got back to me…"

Jane went white as a sheet. "Jesus, no…" But she took the phone when Abbigail offered it. Her head dropped as she started to cry.

Soft, silent, chest-heaving sobs. Abbigail couldn't stand watching Jane break down. Jane had done a lot for her; she couldn't deny it, and she looked like she'd just been sucker punched. She didn't even look angry, just broken and terrified.

"Jane…"

The sheriff put up a hand to stop her. "No, not now." She pushed herself up off her desk and stared down at her with red, tearful eyes. "You're going to go, aren't you, no matter what I say?"

"I don't think I have a choice," Abbigail softly answered. She didn't have it in her heart to look at Jane as she said this, and so she stared at her muddy shoes. "I can't just give up on Andy. He's all the family I have left, and I can feel it." She meant it, she could, in her heart. She had an empty spot where her mom used to be.

It hurt and ached.

But she didn't have that for Andy.

"I don't think he's gone," Abbigail admitted out loud.

She felt Jane staring. It was like a hot prickle that made the tiny, blond, almost invisible hairs stand up on end with a tingle along her neck and arms.

Finally, Jane sighed. "Goddamnit."

WITHERWIX THE CLOWN

I-95 North, New York, July 14th, 2016 – 12:30 p.m.

Abagail stared out the window. They'd been driving for hours. Trees turned into fields, fields into trees, trees and fields into towns and cities, tollbooths, truck stops, gas stations. All in almost complete silence. It had become a blur of grays, greens, browns, and people.

She was tired.

Bone tired.

Her eyelids were heavy.

Droopy.

Abbigail kept having to will herself into not nodding off, her head bowing in surrender to the losing battle against sleep, then jerking lucidly back up again as she fought it off. She worried that if she fell asleep, Jane would drive them home and handcuff her to her bed until she promised to forget about the Golden Ticket Slasher.

Abbigail leaned her head against the window and chanced a glance at Jane. Her jaw was perpetually clenched and she hadn't looked at Abbigail most of the drive. Both hands tightly gripped the wheel at ten and two. Now and again, she took her right hand off the wheel long enough to scoop her department steel to-go cup from its holder in the seat divider between them, take a sip, sigh, and return the cup to its spot.

Abbigail closed her eyes, steadily caving into the temptation she'd been fighting for the last two hours of the drive. Maybe they were too far from home for Jane to turn back now.

So, she was safe to sleep.

She knew it was a dream. But it felt, smelled, and even tasted real. Abbigail stood ankle-deep in virgin snow in a huge frosted pinewood forest. She could feel the vastness of it, the age of it, as it pressed down all around her.

She was at a crossroads in the trees, a path that cut through the woods in a narrow set of trails that went four separate ways. One went back, one went forward, the others went to her left and right, and she stood smack dab in the center. Her breath fogged as it left her nose.

There were signs. Painted ones hammered onto some of the trees, but none of them were helpful. Each one had an arrow of wood pointing one way or the other, and none of them made sense. All of them said the same thing:

Nowhere & Everywhere

"Well, I can't just stay here, so…" She didn't like the look of going back. Somehow, that felt wrong, and right and left looked off, so why not forward? Forward just seemed right. She had a good feeling about going forward, and there was a pleasantness in the air that blew from down that way.

She breathed in a sigh and expelled it with a puff of mist from her lips. The Christmas-y smell of wintergreen was heavy in the air, but so was something else. Something that didn't belong, something that was out of place. It was just a hint, a tease of sweetness. She sniffed at it. It was nice, heartwarmingly pleasant, but she shivered. It was winter here, after all. She was cold, painfully so—and then not.

Abbigail looked down at her new attire of a puffy pink coat. She remembered it; she had had one just like it when she was thirteen, a birthday present from her mom. Sally hadn't wanted Abbigail to know she'd worked lots of overtime to afford it, but she had been so happy watching her open it up.

It was warm. Nostalgia warm. Cozy, like a safe memory. She crossed her arms over her chest and cast about. It should have been pitch black, as it was obviously night in this dream. The silvery light from a full moon hanging low over the trees shone down, glistening off the crystalline-specked snow all about her like a billion disco balls in the dark. Snow-swept pines swayed in the wind.

The moon seemed to be more than a moon. She kept looking up at it, and it seemed, in its own way, to be looking down on her. The shadows and craters on its luminous, craggy surface played tricks on her eyes, giving it a face that seemed to be frowning, glowering contemplatively down from its spot, high, high up. There was nowhere to hide from it. It saw what its light touched, and its light touched everything. Abbigail cast furtive glances up to it, and the further she walked through the woods, braced against the howling winds that rattled the branches of the trees, the less unfriendly it seemed.

It was a loathsome place, pretty, with the glitter of diamonds in the snowy dunes. Yet wickedly cold, bitter, bitter to the bone. And the woods that crept in, gathered about the trail she walked, like lurking monsters, they gave her pause.

Yet, on she went.

She walked, each step crunching and digging deep into the thick, shining powder. Crisp icy crackles and cracks resounded and echoed painfully loud in the stillness of the forest where only the trees creaking and groaning were heard.

It was tough going.

But it wasn't cold for her.

Her awesome puffy jacket saw to that, and the boots, her furry purple princess boots. She followed her nose.

She had no idea where that idea came from, but it was working—or so she hoped—as she soldiered on, bent against the blowing wind that brought with it icy pinpricks that nipped and bit at her face like bugs.

Her mom's fuzzy pink earmuffs kept her ears warm, but they didn't block out the laughter.

She stopped dead.

It wasn't scary. It sounded like children, running through the woods. Her mind whirled as memories flooded in. She and her friends packed snowballs in their mittened hands during a wonderful snow day, pelting each other, peals of laughter ringing in the air. One friend had lost a tooth. A nasty ice ball had smacked it right out of her and sent her sobbing to the ground. Abbigail could see it happening. Like ghosts in the woods, projections of the past played out like ghosts as she rushed to Emily Winters and checked on her. She had been so scared…

Then it was gone, and she felt…empty, lighter, like something had been sucked away, vanished, leaving her less burdened, less *her*, less… Just—less. The passage through the snow grew more burdensome, fighting through the drifts that got deeper and deeper after each step left her more bewildered and tired.

Ahead there played a shimmering boy. "Hey, big sis!" he kept yelling with a huge smile as he ran from her, blasting her with his neon green water gun as he went.

Then it was gone.

Abbigail's head went fuzzy. Like she'd had too much cough medicine. A weird buzzing in her ears accompanying it only added to the discomfort and disorientation as she tried to remember things. Simple things, things she knew were there a short time ago but couldn't find. Like when she put down a remote control, then looked back after a moment and found it wasn't where she'd left it.

It was like an itch she couldn't scratch, a name she knew but couldn't quite visualize enough to say it. She sighed. Knowing she knew something but not what it was or why she'd lost it wasn't fun.

She stared out into the trees. They looked angry, laughing, mocking her with their torturesome creaks and groans, their branches pointing at her like gnarled hands.

Why was she here?

She couldn't remember.

It was there, but too far away to see. A memory blurred by time's passage and long repression that wasn't where or what you recalled it to be.

Had she always been here?

Her eyes burned with tears. She fought it.

"Big girls don't cry," a ghost with a kind, familiar voice reminded her. *"Big girls take life by the horns and kick it in the balls."*

She giggled. But still, the tears came. They froze on her cheeks.

Her breath was mist and fog, cold and shiver-inducing as her teeth chattered, on the verge of tears. She didn't understand why she had stopped. Why was she standing there staring through the icy, howling gusts of snowy wind?

She went on, walking, then pausing, wondering why she had stopped again… Each one, each time, becoming less and less herself as she wandered the woods. Following the growing sweetness blowing in with the breeze. Until it wasn't just wintergreen, it was so much more, but she couldn't define it, she didn't know where she was.

And she was struggling to remember her own name as she pushed forward on tiny legs through the deep heaps of white, fighting the flurries that blued her face and left her tired and hungry.

She had no idea how long she had been walking, only that she had to find the source of the wonderful smell. She knew that would make everything better.

So, on and on she went.

All the trees looked the same, groaning and gnarled things of sap, and stoney browns and grays and whites of snow where bark met winter ice.

The knots, though—she noticed them the longer she walked, and the more she noticed them the faster she went, as they looked like faces in the trees, terrible, misshapen, watching. The shadows of their branches reached for her as they swayed in the wind

A loud sound rumbled in the distance. It wasn't frightening. Just a murmur in the wind that hinted at games, the thunder of rollercoasters…

She tried not to look at the faces in the trees. They were everywhere now. Who did she call for? Was there a thing called Mother? What was it? Would it keep her safe? Was that what people did when they were scared, call for the one called "Mommy"?

Maybe…

Only one way to find out, she supposed. So, she called for it. Again and again. But there was no answer. Nothing but the howl of the wind and her shouts eerily echoing amid the weird, misshapen forest.

Then she saw him.

Standing in the snow

A clown.

She stopped.

What a strange thing.

He was oddly bigger up top than his thin legs seemed able to support. He had tufts of fluffy white hair at the sides and back of his head while the bald section donned a black pointy hat that drooped at the top under the weight of his big, fluffy red pompom. Which, of course, matched his neck ruffles, huge shoes, lips, and nose. His suit was all big black and white diamonds, with more pompoms instead of buttons.

Silent and still, he stared back at her with a set of huge cat's eyes set deep in sunken sockets amid black-painted hollows and lines. The markings went up to his forehead and down to his sharp cheekbones in a face as white as the snow that surrounded them.

He smiled.

The kind of smile that lit up everything about it as he waved to her.

"Hello, Abbigail Hobbs. A-bby… A-bby A-bby…" It greeted her with a nasally, breathy voice that hinted at fairy tales, jokes, and endless laughter. A conglomeration of so many voices melted together to become its own.

"That's my name!" Her face broke into a wide smile as she jumped up and down and clapped her hands. "I couldn't remember, but you did! That's so funny. Does that mean you're my friend?"

"Oh yes, A-bby." It smiled toothily. The way it spoke, its shiny, rubbery red lips over emphasizing each word, it amused. "We are most definitely your one and only, truly, most specialist friend."

Abbigail laughed. "Friends share names. So, what's yours?"

"We are Witherwix the clown," it introduced itself with a silly flourish and spin that merrily rang of bells from its floppy hat and funny squeaks from its huge shoes. "And we were wondering why you are wandering the wicked woods, as it is a bad, bad…bad place, no place at all, for a sweet little girl like you. Tell us, A-bby, tell Witherwix, are you lost?"

A feeling of fear washed over her for a moment like hot water as she looked up at him and got an icky, sick notion…like he was something wrong, awful and wicked, but then it was gone.

She hoped the poor clown, her clown, hadn't seen her fear because it might've hurt his feelings, and that would be mean. And it wasn't nice to be mean to friends.

And he looked so cute.

So funny.

Like a cartoon.

He was huge.

Tall.

Smiley.

In fact, Witherwix seemed instantly friendly, a friend you knew on sight, one you trusted with a wink and smile. She liked him. He made her feel safe and warm. He'd said they were friends, and clowns never lied about such things. That was just a fact all kids knew.

"I don't know," she admitted.

"Ah." Witherwix nodded sagely. "Are you perhaps looking for playmates, sweet, kind, innocent A-bby?"

She smiled at that.

It sounded right on the nose, a nose like the big, red squeaky one the clown had on his silly painted face.

"Sensational, simply marvelous," Witherwix cheered. "As luck would have it, we are the guide for all the good boys and girls to Super Happy Fun Land. Have you heard of it?"

Had she?

Super Happy Fun Land…

It sounded like something she knew.

It sounded right. No, *just right*, so perfectly right that it was as right as rain.

She nodded.

Witherwix gleefully giggled as he danced about, gliding on the snow instead of through it like his big shoes were skis. "Simply splendid!" He paused and put a hand to his ear, listening to whispers in the wind. "Oh…we hear, little one…" In a blink, one moment he was one place, then the next he was right before her, his massive form making her feel so small. "…that perhaps you know someone in Super Happy Fun Land? Is this so?"

A little boy flashed into her mind.

"Andy," she said. "His name is Andy."

"Ah." Witherwix smiled. "Yes, oh yes, An-dy… An-dy, a boy about this tall?" He lifted his hand a little smaller than her, and she nodded. "And with shiny blond hair and the brightest blue eyes, like glass marbles that shine in the moonlight?"

"Yes!"

"We must be sure, as there are ever so many good children in Super Happy Fun Land, so let's see, does An-dy also like spaceships and ice cream…rocky road, with whipped cream and gummy worms? Does he simply love green jellybeans?"

Abbigail laughed and jumped up and down. She could picture Andy in her mind as he spoke. This seemed to delight Witherwix as he nodded and laughed along with her, patting her happily on the head with his huge, white-gloved hand.

"Ah, we know An-dy well and would love to bring you together to play! But…we are afraid you don't yet have a golden ticket… So, you can't get in."

Witherwix put his hands over his face and sobbed, big tears falling to the snow and melting it with steaming hisses as each drop touched down upon it. "We are so sorry, kind, wonderful, beautiful A-bby… Poor Witherwix, the poor sad clown that we are, we can't let you in without one. Whoever heard of anyone getting into Super Happy Fun Land to play without their very own shiny golden ticket?"

She hugged the clown's skinny leg.

He was warm and squishy like a marshmallow and smelled of popcorn and cotton candy.

"It's okay, Witherwix. Don't be sad! How can I get a golden ticket? I'm sure I can find one…"

"Oh…" His sobbing stopped, and he hugged her back. "Well, you would have to be a super-duper ice cream sundae sweet and nice. And you are, so one box checked…" He ticked this off by folding down a finger on one red frilly-cuffed hand.

Then he frowned.

And all the world seemed dark and sad as his face shadowed and tears brimmed in his eyes. "But then, a payment must be made, a Mommy would pay it for you. Tell us, pretty, sweet, kindly, A-bby, do you have a Mommy?"

"I don't know…" She remembered calling for a mommy.

But no one came.

No one at all.

Perhaps she didn't have one?

Or lost the one that was hers?

The very thought hurt to think about.

Witherwix's frown deepened.

His big eyes glowed brightly.

Like Christmas-light green.

"Hmmm… Let us see." Witherwix put his finger to her forehead and hummed a circus tune, pretty and cheerful. "Oh, poor Witherwix sees you've lost her, shame, shame, shame… But fear not, as we know that a mommy isn't a mommy by blood alone. So yes, yes, yes. Sweet, kind, pretty A-bby—we shall see about payment, and then…"

He held her at arm's length and smiled down at her.

"Then the real fun begins."

Abbigail awoke with a start, tears in her eyes, and classic rock on the radio. It was dark, very dark.

"You've been out for a while," Jane said from the front seat. "You okay, hon?"

Abbigail sat up. She felt rested but oddly still tired. "Yeah. I had the weirdest dream…" She trailed off as she wiped the sleep crust from her eyes, mind foggy as she tried to pick out what she had been dreaming about.

"Oh, really?" Jane cast a glance over her shoulder with an arched brow before turning back to the road. "What about?"

"I don't remember." Abbigail shook her head, vague echoes stirring in the fog of her memory that hinted at happiness, snow, and…what else? It was there, right out of reach, at the very tip of her tongue, just far enough away that she could see its vague outline, but not what it was. "It was snowing…" she muttered with a shrug. "That's it, that's all I've got."

"You hate snow."

"I didn't always." Abbigail smiled then sighed as guilt weighed on her. "I've said some things…"

"Stop, kid." Jane smiled at her sadly in the rear-view mirror. "I know, I get it, it's okay."

"Thanks." Abbigail smiled back at her, and suddenly things didn't seem so dark. "For everything."

THE CIRCUS AT WORLD'S END

Carnival Way, New York, July 15th, 2016

"Jesus," Jane gasped as they drove into town, passing by a man on stilts in a gray tuxedo and huge hat atop a mop of curly green hair that he doffed and bowed as they passed. He had a blue smile, a white painted face, blue makeup circles about his eyes, and he honked a large silver horn as they slowly left him to their bumper.

Abbigail stared after the man. Then gawked at a trio on the opposite side of the sidewalk. One, a painfully thin woman, did flips in tight silver gymnast wear. Easily keeping pace with a shirtless, heavily tattooed bald man with a beard and leather pants and boots who was juggling bowling ball pins. The last of the trio was a very small clown with a rainbow wig and a white jumpsuit splattered with polka-dots in every color. He carried a huge boombox on his shoulder that was blasting *'The Electric Slide'* on what had to be the highest volume. Jane's car rattled from the bass.

The houses were nicer than the pictures; old, sure, but the chipped paint clapboards were accented with new windows done in bright colors. Colors splashing all over lawns that were more flower than grass. But it was weird, like a place where only half existed sanely. There were grandfather clocks in the yards. Ticking away. One house with a lavishly lavender painted door had a llama in a tartan vest with a huge carnation pinned to its breast pocket tethered in a front lawn, grazing on a hay bale. It watched them curiously as they drove past its yard.

"Holy shit…" Abbigail's eyes went wide. An elephant, huge and gray with massive white tusks, lumbered along the road. It had a collar on. A pink one. Bejeweled with shiny stones that flashed in the sunlight. It had a ridiculously insufficient leash, held by a clown with pink cheeks dressed in a pink, sparkly ballerina dress and camo jacket dancing her way along the road. She glared at them as they passed. The elephant trumpeted as though it shared its ballerina friend's opinion of them being trespassers.

The rows of houses ended, and as they crossed a gaggle of teenagers in clown suits of varying colors and a man in a sleeveless tux jacket and top hat walking a lion like a Labrador, they were drawn by a sight that they couldn't look away from. Sprawled across the massive cornfield ahead lay all the carnival rides, all the big tops, all the game booths hawking goldfish for glass bottle ring tosses, all the circus attractions in the world.

Before the field stood a big florescent green sign that read:

Welcome to World's End Farm, where every season of fun begins & ends.

"Well, that sounds cheerful. Not creepy at all," Jane remarked, eyeing the sign that was being cleaned by a muscular bearded man with a long squeegee.

The music in the car went dead as they approached the field, fuzzing out with a blasting sharp and sudden burst of static, then changing into pipe organ circus music—the same tune that was blaring out of the massive carnival, or whatever it was that was stretched across the field. It changed so abruptly that it made Jane jump in her driver's seat. Abbigail stared. She couldn't help herself. As they passed row after row of shiny silver Airstream trailers about which carnies congregated around coolers of beer and campfires in denim vests, tight jeans, handlebar mustaches, mullets, and cowboy boots. They all paused in their animated conversation to watch them drive by. Even a huge oiled-up man and woman, wearing matching leopard print bikini bottoms as they lifted weights outside their shiny silver trailer, noticed them driving by. The man, who had a shaved head and the most spectacular waxed mustache Abbigail had ever seen, dropped his monstrous dumbbells. He put his ham-sized fists on his hips as his partner restarted her workout. Doing curls and making uncomfortable eye contact with Abbigail as she stared back at them from the window of Jane's car.

Abbigail had never felt so out of place and uncomfortable in her whole life. The looks they were getting stated plainly they weren't welcome, that they were outsiders. Sticking out like a sore thumb.

Horses were tethered outside of buildings. There were colorful people on unicycles, big-wheeled bikes straight out of the early eighteen hundreds, one person riding a camel…but very little in the way of car parking. Golf carts, Segways, and scooters galore. But it took close to ten minutes to find a place to stop. They were guided in like they were landing a fighter jet on an aircraft carrier by a mime with a pair of blue Mets baseball pennants on sticks.

"I'm going to regret this," Jane breathed as she watched the white-faced mime in his tight black and white shirt spin and swing about her car like he was ballroom dancing with a lovely lady that no one could see. "I really am…"

Abbigail didn't know what to say. Heat battered her as she got out of the car, listening to a mix of crickets chirping away and carnival music. She stepped out and discovered a little bald man in a business suit with shiny brown loafers waiting. He wore a monocle and held a shiny black wooden cane topped with an ivory elephant's head, which he leaned on while staring impatiently at a golden pocket watch. All at once, Abbigail thought of the white rabbit from her mom's favorite fairy tale and wondered with a deep feeling of unease how far down the rabbit hole this trip was going to take her.

"Abbigail Hobbs?" he asked in a tiny yet deep voice as he irritably snapped shut his pocket watch and stuffed it into his vest's pocket, leaving only the shiny chain hooked to the vest's very top ivory button dangling down.

How could he wear that in this heat? It wasn't just hot; it was oppressive, like standing by the oven in a pizza parlor, sweaty in awful places, an itchy kind of hot. She wondered about all this as she peered down at him and he up at her.

"Yes…" Abbigail stepped forward, and the little man squinted up at her with very dark eyes that looked almost black, but they were blue, and sparks of it shone in the sunlight.

"This way, please." Without another word, he hobbled off with a very defined limp. Then, he stopped and spun so suddenly that Jane ran right into the rubber tip of his cane that he held out like a sword and stared down at him with shock as he shook his head.

"No spares."

"I'm her—" Jane started, then frowned as the man shook his head.

"Are you related?" he demanded.

"Well," Jane eyed Abbigail helplessly, and the man sighed.

"*Well,* is not related. We haven't much time, no time at all, for spares. Bobo's time is precious. And he wants to see her," he pointed at Abbigail with his cane, "not spares. If you don't like it, you can both leave."

"Fine," Jane started, then sighed as Abbigail glared at her and shook her head. "Fine," she repeated, but this time it was a surrender.

"I'll be okay. You've got nothing to worry about," Abbigail assured her, and Jane bit her lip and stared first at her, then at the little man in his suit, then breathed out another defeated sigh.

"Great. What do I do 'til you get back?"

The little man pointed to the carnival with his cane, particularly to the admissions booth manned by a blue clown holding a leashed piglet wearing a sparkly pink tutu.

"Explore, play." He turned his back on her, then paused and said over his shoulder, "But be mindful, this is our world, and a little respect here goes a long way."

Jane eyed the carnival, unsure, and her face told a story of being deeply unnerved by the prospect of wandering the massive fairground alone. She gave Abbigail a resigned wave. "Find me when you get back."

Abbigail followed the little man; he was shockingly nimble for one with such a painfully pronounced limp who ambulated with a cane. He easily outpaced her as he led her up a pristine, flower-bordered cement slab sidewalk to a big brick building next to an even bigger red brick building.

It was the museum. It was hard to miss, as it had a massive fountain out front with three clowns and an elephant in a pool. The clowns squirted water from flowers on their lapels, and the elephant on its hind legs sprayed from its trunk.

She was sweating already and she'd only been walking, what? Ten minutes?

The smell of the carnival was heavy on the unnaturally still, humid air. They ascended a set of four cement steps that led to a pair of tall glass doors large enough to admit an elephant, which her guide irritably held open for her. Not in a polite way. But in an *I don't have time for this slow, gawky girl* sort of way.

She stepped into the smaller building and was blasted by a gust of chilled air-conditioning. It raised gooseflesh on her arms.

Manikins, white, faceless, life-sized dolls, wearing old wigs and clown suits, stood in glass cases along the hall, in a long, incredibly creepy row. Each one had a brass plate denoting its owner and their dates of birth and death. There were even pictures mounted above some of the displays. Abbigail didn't understand why, but it made her sad to look at them. Their footfalls and his cane taps echoed on the black-and-white checkered tile floor. It was so shiny and clean that she could see the displays even when she looked down.

"Here we are." The little man stopped before a set of huge double doors with handles shaped like clown heads and rapped on the cherry-wood sharply with his cane.

"Enter," a soft, raspy voice, barely audible through the wood, called from beyond the doors.

"After you." The little one smiled and, hesitantly, Abbigail set forward with a sigh of resignation and grabbed the handle. She gasped. It was cold. Ice cold. She yanked her fingers away, rubbing at her hand as the man smiled.

"Go on." He nodded at the door. "You've come all this way, haven't you? Why would you stop now?"

He was right. Abbigail slowly took the handle again. It wasn't cold anymore. Cool, yes, but not the skin-numbing chill that had shocked her when first she had grabbed ahold of it.

The little man chuckled as she turned the knob and pushed. It didn't move a bit, so she pulled it, and with a groan, the door opened with unexpected ease into a surprisingly small room, much longer than it was wide. After another glance at the creepily smiling small man, she stepped inside.

A skeleton of a man in a tweed suit with an oversized red bowtie sat behind a desk at the far end of the office.

He had clown makeup on, because of course he did, and he was wearing a plastic mask attached to tubes. The hissing and puffing of an oxygen machine was the only sound in the library-like hall of a bookish room. The old man, who had red circles painted about his eyes, peered at her over the rims of tiny gold round glasses.

"Thank you, Mayor Tallfoot," he said, and the little man bowed to him like he was royalty, then backed out of the room, closing the door with a slow groan as he left them to talk. The door shut with a startling *BOOM* of finality that shivered on into silence as the old clown and Abbigail studied one another.

"Abbigail Hobbs." He smiled. His teeth were brown and twisted. "I am Bobo. Thank you for being punctual. I've had my cards read just this morning and we've not much time, so please." He pointed to his desk. "Bring me the ticket."

Abbigail stared at the sad old clown. What had he meant by having his cards read, she wondered. Like fortune tellers' kind of Tarot cards in the dark with fake crystal balls and palm-reading bullshit? She decided she didn't want to know. She felt uneasy, like she was in a crypt looking at a corpse that hadn't been boxed up yet as he expectantly peered up at her, each breath a shuddering rasp fogging up the clear plastic of his oxygen mask. Abbigail walked up to the desk, eying row after row of wooden shelves full of books, ancient-looking photo albums, circus props, creepy masks, and jarred things floating in green fluids lit up by overhead lamps that made her skin crawl. Withdrawing the golden ticket from her pocket as she came to a stop, she then placed it before the old clown. He eagerly snatched it up in arthritically clawed, trembling fingers and brought it close to his face.

He squinted at it, turning it this way and that, then flipped it over and did it all over again. "It's genuine," he sighed. "And while it's not the first, and won't be the last, it is the final one these old eyes shall see."

"You know what it is?"

"Of course."

"You know who left it?"

"Not personally." Bobo chuckled darkly, choking and coughing with the effort answering had taken. "But yes. And no. It's not a *who,* exactly, more of a *they.* Perhaps it is more accurate to say that they are a *what,* that both is and isn't."

What was that supposed to mean? This beef jerky of a shriveled-up old clown was her last and only hope, so she choked back her seething impatience and took a steady breath. "Please tell me. Is my brother… Can he be saved?"

"What is claimed by Super Happy Fun Land cannot be reclaimed by this world." The old clown shook his head. "It is all lost to nowhere, and the road to everywhere is past the veil of life and dreams… So those who walk it cannot go back."

She didn't believe him, and she didn't understand him, so she asked, "What is it?"

"Super Happy Fun Land?" Bobo curiously cocked his head to the side, and she nodded. He frowned, his makeup accentuating the sad look.

"No one knows for sure." Bobo shrugged. "Some say it's heaven. Others say it's…well, something else."

"Heaven?"

"For some." Bobo nodded, his eyes wide and glistening with something like faith. "What do you think heaven looks like…to *us?*"

Abbigail looked uneasily at him.

"Harps and white robes?" Bobo asked in a trembling voice. "Or big tops and roller coasters, with laughter and kettle corn popping while children play?"

Horror filled Abbigail as she gaped at the dying clown. He smiled sadly back at her. "And what would our heaven need to be filled with to be heaven? For us, those who lived for laughter and games and play?"

Abbigail felt sick.

"Say it," Bobo demanded.

"It would need to be filled with children…" Abbigail's eyes filled with tears.

"Correct. And for one to pass to everywhere, another must first pass on to nowhere to pay the admission, or that heaven would be empty…"

Abbigail let out a sob into her hand. "Oh… God."

Each word the old clown uttered was a nauseating twist of a knife in her gut. But despite her revulsion and tears, she kept listening.

"Not quite," Bobo mused. "But as I said, it is what *some* believe."

Abbigail knew just by looking that Bobo was one of *them*, even if he wouldn't admit it.

"And the Slasher?" Abbigail demanded, pushing forward even though she was terrified of what kind of demented answer she would get. "The Golden Ticket Slasher, what is he?"

"A demon to some… An angel to others."

Of all the answers she expected, that was worse and entirely outside of the realm of anything she had expected to hear. It was sick, depraved. Wicked.

"Golden Ticket Slasher…" Bobo chuckled. "Silly, but accurate… I suppose. But his proper name is Witherwix. And before you ask, he is older than our knowledge of him, and no one really knows what he truly is. But that is not important. What is…" He choked and coughed. It took a moment to regain his composure. "…is that, what Witherwix takes, Witherwix keeps. No takesey-backsies, no negotiation, no exceptions."

"There has to be a way."

"There isn't. I am sorry. Your brother can never walk again in the world of the living."

"So, he's dead?" Abbigail gasped, tears brimming. "Is that what you're saying?"

"To *you*, yes. And there is no way to bring him back, none at all, and before you ask it, there's also no way to stop Witherwix from his work. He isn't of this world, not really."

"And if I try to find a way?" she asked.

"You wouldn't be the first to try," said Bobo. "Should you search for what you've lost, a path will open to you, one that you may not wish to walk, and one that you will not walk alone. Beware, child, for should you seek, he will find, and then you will join…the others."

"Others?" She shivered, wondering how the hellish nightmare she was stuck in could get any worse.

"Oh, yes." Bobo sighed; he looked pained by more than his waning mortality. "There are legends, rumors of a place, a terrible place where Witherwix plants the souls of those it deems… unworthy."

Abbigail hadn't been ready for that. She folded her arms over her chest as a sick, clammy feeling swept through her. "So, if I try to stop him, or I try to go after my brother to bring him back?"

"Witherwix will protect Super Happy Fun Land," Bobo warningly answered in a warbling voice, "and most likely, he will carve from you your brightness, your very soul. And you shall become another damned, twisted denizen of the bad place that rings the land of eternal play."

Abbigail wanted to puke.

"I'm sorry if this news isn't what you hoped to hear," Bobo continued. "I am truly sorry."

Abbigail didn't believe him. No, he was holding something back, something awful and vital as he stared up at her with a sad clown face.

"You won't help me. You could. But you won't, will you?"

"I can, I have. I've told you the truth, my child. And now, to dissuade you from your quest, I will show it to you." He rang a tiny silver bell on his desk, and at once the door opened and Mayor Tallfoot stepped back in.

"You rang, Bobo?" the diminutive man respectfully inquired. Abbigail's skin crawled to see the way the little man stared with bubbling awe and brimming respect at Bobo, shriveled and withered to all but skin and bone in his wheelchair, struggling to find the strength to answer.

"Take this." Bobo laboriously slid the gleaming golden ticket forward to Abbigail. "And, my good mayor, if you would be so kind… Please, show our guest to the hall of lament."

It was a short walk, through a door, downstairs, into a small room. There was a single table and chair set on a red cream tasseled rug. On the polished, round wood tabletop sat a box of tissues, a corked whiskey bottle, a single shot glass, and a pink glass vase of flowers. The room itself was well-lit, cold, simple gray cement, the walls unadorned, and the only change to it was a door like one would open to step into an ordinary house.

"Here." The mayor produced a tack, a bright red plastic-topped one from a golden pillbox he had full of them in his pleated trousers pocket. She took it, confused, and more than a little unnerved. The mayor smiled, pointing at the door. "Go on."

She approached, eyeing the table, the whiskey, and the tissues uneasily as she passed them and got to the door. The doorknob was icy cold. Just like the one to Bobo's office had been.

She gripped it. Looked over her shoulder at Mayor Tallfoot, who was leaning with both hands onto his cane, silently watching her.

"What's in there?" she asked.

"What you're looking for, of course." He shrugged. "The truth."

With little other choice, Abbigail pushed open the door. Out came a howling gust of cold, so vicious and brutal that she backed away, allowing the door to crash loudly against the wall. She gagged at the awful stink of it that cloyingly clung to her senses, choking her to a fit of coughs as she doubled over and covered her nose and mouth with her clammy, trembling hands. It was like rotting apples and death. Chest heaving and skin prickling, she pushed in, shocked that the wind was all but gone in the long, arched, gloomily lit tunnel of gray stone.

The lights flickered as she stepped into the ankle-deep mire of eddying fog blanketing the floor. Milky-white tendrils of it flitted ethereally towards her like tiny ghostly hands. Reaching to drag her down.

The foul-smelling gusts went in and out, in and out. Like the hall was the throat of a long, vile, eternally hungry serpent. One that was feeding on the death and misery each ticket represented. It was oppressive, claustrophobic, and terrifying. Every moment she stood there felt like an eternity of suffering. She was dissolving, coming apart, slowly and agonizingly digested. But that wasn't the worst part.

Abbigail's legs folded underneath her, dropping her painfully to her knees.

There were so many, tacked to the walls, rustling like autumn leaves with each gust.

An endless gloomy hall lined with golden tickets as far as the eye could see.

Jane paid the admission of twenty dollars to the silent, smiling clown who merely pointed to the sign denoting the cost of entry. He took the crisp bill then theatrically bowed her onwards amid a peel of unnervingly gleeful giggles. She stepped past the entry arch and onto the yellow brick path to the fair. Or whatever it was.

The music came from everywhere, as did the smells. It was like it was being piped in, pumped into the air. Hotdogs, sweet candy, fried foods, and popped corn blasted in and hung like an ethereal fog throughout the loud rows of booths and tents. Clowns, men who looked like drifters in ratty old jeans and patch-covered vests, and others in outlandish performer costumes, young and old, were everywhere. Playing, popping balloons with darts. Climbing rope ladders to claim prizes. Throwing balls at dunk tank targets. Hands in the air, screaming their lungs empty on rides that spun and dropped…

And still more worked the countless booths, games, attractions, and rides, calling out with bullhorns and talking into microphones attached to speakers.

It was overwhelming.

The noise.

The smells.

The sights.

Jane aimlessly wandered past funnel cake vendors, nacho cheese and chip carts, ice cream trucks…

Her belly growled.

Her arms crossed over her chest, Jane unexpectedly found herself hungrily eying a hotdog cart. It smelled divine: chili, onions, steamed dogs… They called to her. Like in the old cartoons, where fragrant steam wafting off of something delicious quite literally beckoned in a hungry character. Reeling them floatingly to the feast in a dreamy haze of hunger.

Her belly insisted she stop.

She wandered over and waited in line. It was busy but quick. The smiling old-timer, with each finger ringed in silver and turquoise and a black cowboy hat and jeans, whipped out hotdogs and ice-cold cans of soda pop from a cooler cart at an impressive pace.

"First Gathering?" he asked Jane in a two-pack of cigarettes a day, deep, growly rasp as he plucked a dog out of the steamroller with a pair of tongs and put it on a bun that he held in a paper serving cozy.

"What now—?"

"Gathering." The old man eyed her from under his hat brim with piercing blue eyes, his gray mustache twitching. "Oh, I see… You're with *her*."

"Who?" Jane narrowly eyed him.

"We all know." The old cowboy shrugged while he deftly settled the fragrantly steaming hotdog into the roll. "Chili?"

"Sure." Jane blinked. "You all know what, exactly?"

Chuckling, he ladled thick, rich, meaty chili onto the dog. "The girl with the golden ticket. You're here with her? Aren't y'all?"

Ice climbed up Jane's spine as the old cowboy pointed to the condiments meticulously organized on his cart. "Relish, onion, mustard, and cheese? Sound bout right, ma'am?"

She stared, and her belly growled. "Yes, please."

"We have this each year, the Gathering," he went on as he scooped onions. "Even we need to blow off steam, and what better way than this?" He chuckled as he put a wiggly yellow line of mustard onto the dog. "Every year, at least one outsider shows up, like clockwork. And they all have one thing in common. The golden tickets." With a satisfied sigh, the old cowboy added a liberal dash of relish to his hotdog masterpiece and handed it over.

She took it and stared, unsure of what to say.

"And how does it go for them?" she asked.

"Grape soda, ma'am?" he asked instead of coughing up an answer to her question, which he seemed to prefer to ignore. "You look like the kinda gal who liked grape soda as a kid, am I right? I usually am."

"I'd love that…" She nodded as he handed one over even before she spoke; it was so cold, drips of icy water and condensation frosting the purple can. Familiar. The one her mom used to buy. The exact one.

She hadn't seen it in years.

Not anywhere.

Her mouth ached for it.

"On the house, ma'am. Enjoy." He tipped his hat to her and scooped up a bun in a cozy and had his tongs snatching up another dog for the clown waiting patiently behind her.

She stepped out of line, took a bite of her hotdog, and stopped dead. It was perfect, the chili. She hadn't tasted the likes of it in years; it was just like her grandpa used to make. *"No damned beans,"* he used to say as he stirred the pot. *"Should be hot and meaty, not beany."*

It was perfect. She glanced back at the hotdog vendor cart. To her unease, several of the other customers waiting in line to be served were staring right at her. But they all quickly looked away as soon as she saw them looking.

She headed along the path to the games, idly watching kid

clowns and teenagers throw softballs at stacks of wooden milk bottle targets and shoot hoops with basketballs for stuffed prizes.

Balloons popped sharply.

BB guns cracked.

Bells rang.

Balls rumbled along Skee-ball tracks.

They all seemed to have just as much luck as everyone else did, losing more than they won. Even so, they had just as much fun as everyone who had ever played. Jane found herself smiling despite her gnawing worry, eating her hotdog and sipping her drink as the heat beat down like the sun was just feet away.

She stopped when she saw a big setup ahead. She knew it. She must have, because it stank of nostalgia, a two-trailer attraction painted black and speckled with scary green faces that, by the looks of it, glowed in the dark. Its entry was up a set of black metal steps leading through the mouth of a laughing clown wearing a red propeller hat. You had to step over its bottom teeth and duck to avoid the top teeth to get in. Its loud, clownish laughter mesmerized her. Its eyes moved with each laugh, clicking wide one way then the other as the man in the black suit with the pointy pencil mustache dared, "One and all to walk up, step up, and brave the road to nowhere though *Doctor Draco's Funhouse of Evil*," through his megaphone.

Yes. Jane could've sworn she'd seen this before. She finished her hotdog, licking the chili and mustard from her fingers and tossing the crumpled paper into the mouth of the novelty clown trashcan as she tried to remember when and where she would've encountered such a place. Maybe she was imagining things. She was about to walk away when the attraction attendant noticed her. "I see you there, outsider. Come on then, give Doctor Draco's Funhouse of Evil a go, what do you say? For you, it's free! What do you have to lose?"

Jane shook her head and put up her hands in a comical way that made him laugh as everyone nearby turned to watch.

"Oh, come on now, don't be afraid. Millions have gone before you, and millions more will go after you, be a sport. Walk the walk. We have such amazing, spine-tingling things to show you in the horrible halls of Doctor Draco's Funhouse of Evil!"

The onlookers laughed.

Jane did, too, but still, she waved it off to a mocking "Bock, bock, bock, bock" from the attendant as he flapped his arms like chicken wings. "Come on, outsider, this is where the real fun begins!"

She blushed furiously and then made her way to the steps up to the attendant.

"Ah, there we go, found your courage, eh?" He gestured to the clown's mouth with a wolfish smile. "Welcome. Step on in." He eyed her with a sardonic carney malevolence, an act he had obviously long perfected as he fluffed his costume cape and doffed his top hat with a flourishing bow. "Don't touch anything, and remember, there are no exits for scaredy-pants. Once in, there's only one way out."

Jane laughed, nervous, and ducked in—then, in a sick rush, remembering that she had hated this attraction. She had done it once, only once, the very year Timmy had vanished. Abbigail whirled about as the attendant laughed. A long, high, manic peal of mirth as he stepped on the peddle at his foot and the jaws of the clown's mouth came crashing down.

DOCTOR DRACO'S FUNHOUSE OF EVIL

Carnival Way, New York – The Gathering

Jane's heart raced in her chest like pistons in an engine firing away as she slowly turned back from the blocked entry and eyed the spinning room.

It was a trick of light, yellows and blues twirling about before a single door across a short catwalk. No more than six steps long, locked in a rotating pipe that wound endlessly round and round while the lights flashed and strobed. Distorted, fragmented calliope music played, and clowns' laughter filled the space. Jane leaned on the guardrail and shook her head, trying to clear away the dizzying sensation.

She panted her way forward, hand over hand, to the twisted glowing green door, the only way out. "Shit, shit, shit."

She grabbed the handle and yelped.

It zapped her.

Like one of those bargain prank toys kids love that was worn like a ring to shock friends who went in for the bait of the offered bro handshake.

"God dammit," she snapped as the door creaked open. The next room leaked fog from a smoke machine into the spiny entryway, from a dark place that was full of whispers. It was pitch black. Like so black, she doubted she could see her hand in front of her face if she put it an inch from her nose.

"What choice do I have?" she asked the room, and thankfully, it didn't answer as she stepped into the darkness. The moment she cleared the door, of course, it slammed shut behind her. And it was just as dark as she thought it was going to be.

Jane groaned.

She pushed out her arms, slowly shuffling forward step by step. She remembered this; Timmy had held her hand when they went through it as a group. Brad Cooper, who had died in a car accident the year after they graduated, had been the one to find the exit straight ahead.

First, she heard it.

Whispering.

No clear words.

Just gibberish.

Then laughter.

Like an evil soundtrack of malicious shrieking with hundreds of people all belting out their mockingly sinister mirth at once while she shambled forward.

Then she saw it.

Lights were glowing, illuminating a door ahead of her, shining blue and white through the thin cracks, so close she had almost bumped into it as she fumbled blindly about.

It opened inward automatically at her approach with a very haunted house classic creak as cackles, like a witch in the dark stirring a cauldron, rang out. Chains clanked, haunting groans shivering in the air as Jane apprehensively approached.

This room was thin and lit by a strobe and nothing else, and all of it was mirrors, seamlessly arranged so that it all looked the same 'til you looked at them directly. Then they showed you different "you's"

She stepped in, and predictably, the door shut behind her, vanishing behind its own mirrors as she looked about. She was fat in one, wiggly in another, and tall in the next. Everywhere she turned, she was changed. Even the ceiling was mirrored, and the floor was a foggy cube of reflections refracting bright strobing lights. She didn't see a door or any obvious way out.

The claustrophobia kicked in tenfold as she frantically stared around herself. Then something cold squeezed the air from her lungs as something caught her eye.

It had been in a glance that she'd seen it. A flash that her mind almost dismissed as she'd uneasily swept the creepy ten-step mirrored hall with a hardened gaze. Apprehensively, her heart skipped a beat, stuttering and jumping as it thundered in her chest. She looked again across the mirrors.

She was upside down in one mirror, tiny in another, a beanpole in one more, and then not alone in the next. She was scared to look, but she did. But it was gone, the shape that had been watching her.

Vanished.

Jane sighed in relief and then screamed as she turned around. It was in front of her, tall, grease-painted, white-faced and smiling, glowing eyes staring at her from within circles of black as it raised a butcher's knife over its head. The knife came down in a silvery flash. Jane fell back, throwing herself away from the sharp steel. Her eyes squeezed shut, her hands held up before her.

But nothing happened.

No sharp pain.

No knife digging into her.

Nothing.

Jane raggedly sucked in breath after breath as terror coursed through her, pumping fiery blood that she felt like a buzz as she looked up. A mirror. A fucking goddamned mirror. Another cheap trick.

"Oh, Jesus…" She panted as she slowly regained her bearings, her pulse a crazy train of rapid beats that hammered away at her veins. It was coming back to her now. This room was a mind-bender. The door slid open to her right, leading into more mirrors and strobes. She got up, pushing herself off the floor, then froze again.

It was there, staring at her, feet away. Smiling in a way that made her skin crawl. Knife in one hand and waving to her with the other. She backed away, and it cocked its head, watching, its pompom-tipped floppy hat jingling like it had a bell in it. Then it raised a hand and pointed at her.

Laughing.

It was a terrifying sound.

A nightmarish chorus of distorted voices all mocking her at once, a gallery full of them pointing and cackling like she was a toy to amuse themselves with.

It went on and on as Jane backed away, never blinking.

"It's not real," Jane insisted to herself. "It's just a carnival funhouse… Nothing can hurt me." She steeled herself, then screamed again as she bumped into something.

She whipped about and there it was again, smiling in the mirror.

Staring at her with horrible, hungry eyes.

"Poor Jane Anne Wattson… *Jane-y*," the clown sang.

Jane's insides violently lurched while she recoiled from it.

The way the clown had said her name made her feel like she was falling, plummeting down a twisted rabbit hole of madness. Dropped screaming down a glass tube of lights and mirrors as its head twisted and turned in ways no head had any right to.

"Sheriff Jane-y," it mocked. "She lost Fredd-y and still misses Timm-y and is scared for A-bby... Aww. So cute. So nice. Haha!"

"What the fuck..." Jane scrambled back while it pointed and howled in amusement. Then another one in another mirror did the same, then another and another. The sounds were a cacophony of madness.

"You are wrong, Jane-y," one said, cat eyes flaring wickedly as they went as wide as tennis balls. "This is not a cheap trick. *No. No. No.*" It wagged a huge gloved finger, then pointed it at her and snickered. Like she had just said the funniest joke it had ever heard. While the reflection Jane stared at with wide eyes mocking her pointing her way and unleashing an insane peel of sinister mirth, another started chopping at its side of the mirror with a red-headed axe, white cracks *tinkling* along the glass.

"We are Witherwix the clown," it giggled from another mirror. "And we want Abb-y... Perfect, pretty, innocent, kindly Abb-y... We want to bring her to the special place of forever play: Super Happy Fun Land. Where every breath is a scream of laughter, and every moment is filled with joy for all the good little boys and girls. We want Abb-y to be our most specialist of friends. Just like we wanted Jo-ann-y, An-dy, Tim-my, Keith-y, Bobb-y, Bett-y, Zech-y, Pat-ty, Edd-y, Dann-y, *and so many, many more.*"

Each name was breathed like it was a revered thing. A prayer, a secret, a joy all harshly spat forth in a singsong parody of a voice that wasn't just one, it was so much more.

Jane screamed as another reflection started punching the mirror on its side, making huge, frosted white impact circles in the glass, hammering at it like a boxer who had his man on the ropes.

"But Abbigail will be little Abb-y again, and she shall have a smile from ear to ear, and live forever in the eternal joy and play of Super Happy Fun Land… But first," it smiled in a way no face should be able to contort itself. "First, there is the price of admission."

Glass exploded with a shocking suddenness as bits of mirror rained outward. Out stepped the clown, red shoes squeaking as its massive frame crushed the glass under its feet. An axe in its hands, it pinned her with a glowing gaze that froze her blood solid.

"That's where you come in."

It moved in with an unearthly bellowing that sounded like the gates of hell themselves had been kicked in and all the souls in it were howling for release. Jane clambered forward, the axe head striking the glass where she had been moments before. She raced beneath the thing's long legs to the door just past it.

It whirled about and roared, spittle spraying in foul tendrils that smoked and blackened the glass when they landed on the debris-strewn floor. Its mouth opened like a snake, unhinging as yellow, sharp teeth peeled into view from behind its blood-red lips when it hungrily smiled. Its eyes glowed, flaring with a hellish rage that made her weak in the knees as she struggled to open the door.

Hitting it.

Sobbing with terror while wildly pounding at it.

Punching and slapping it.

Screaming.

Pulling and twisting the handle.

She heard it coming, the thunder of feet on broken glass, hammering, howling, laughing, and then she fell through the door, and it closed just as the axe came down. The silvery edge of the blade and a little red poked through the splintered wood. Then, with a shudder of the door on its hinges, it was yanked back and a terrible glowing green eye peered in at her.

"Don't you want Abb-y to be happy?"

She scrambled back along the floor, heart racing, mind reeling.

"Is not her happiness worth your life to pay for her eternal joy? You can purchase that for her, Jane-y."

"Go away! You can't have her!" Jane screamed, and in answer, it roared, pounding wildly at the door until it shook and shook on its hinges, then abruptly stopped.

"You are already dead, Jane-y. *It's done.* You are for us now. For the delicious pain, like sweet cotton candy, and brightness. It purchases our love and the way to Super Happy Fun Land for A-bby."

Clear as day, she could see its pointy yellow teeth and blood-red lips pressed to the gaping hole as it spoke to her. "Give her admission willingly, and you won't go to the bad place. Mommys who ignore their special girl's happiness makes mommy very, very naughty. *Naughty* is not nice. It gets punished. Forever. I plant their being, their dim brightness, in the wicked woods, and up *pops* their tree. *Up, up, up,* like heated, buttery popping corn."

The way the clown said *naughty,* all watery, wicked, and warbling, made Jane's skin crawl as she glared at it, rage and terror bubbling up in equally volcanic proportions.

"Fuck you!" Jane screamed as she rushed away and up, running for the next door, pushing through the huge plastic bat props dangling from the ceiling. It snarled its rage, striking violently at the door as she ran.

The next exit was a portcullis drawn up with a rattle of chains. The room beyond had more fog in it and was lit with flashing red strobes. Meat hooks hung from the ceiling on chains. So many of them jingling and swaying. She pushed through.

"Oh, Jane-y."

It was there. She felt its breath on her ear, warm, reeking of hotdogs, popcorn, and cotton candy as agony speared her back. She grunted, not even able to cry out as she felt the hook go in, just under her ribs by her spine. The merciless metal hook pushed an awful, gulping grunt from her as she stood there shaking, not sure how she was still standing. Her knees were like Jello, her toes dragging across the funhouse floor, and she sagged while the hook in her ribs and the chain were all that held her upright.

"Why did you have to go and run?" it growled wetly into her ear.

Somehow, horrifically, she hadn't passed out. It was all so clear, so vivid, the pain.

The huge walled industrial fan that was slowly spinning just ahead.

She could see the exit; it was right there.

Under the fan

But she was hooked.

Hooked good.

Hooked deep.

"That was very, very *naughty*," the clown rumbled as it yanked at the chain, jerking her off her feet with one hard pull after another until she hung there just a little higher up than the clown. "*Naughty girls get punished.*"

Jane had no control over her hands. She tried to struggle, but the pain was too much. She stared down at the hook protruding from her body. The blood was coppery, like sucking on a mouthful of old pennies, as it burbled wetly out of her lips as she choked out breath after agonizing breath. Her body involuntarily twitched, spasming and jerking. Like a fish fighting the line that was reeling it in, her mind was left burning with a fire of agony as she swayed there from the hook. Dangling like a prized trout, the clown catch of the day.

Blood seeped down her face. It tasted like she was sucking on a copper pipe. A bitter, metallic resonance that her body fought with torturous, bile-filled, heaves as slowly, agonizingly, she went numb.

Jane could feel the hook there, inside her, agony, ice. Slicing outward and inward with a chill freezing her from the inside out.

The clown leered with its hideous red lips.

She tried to spit at it, tried to curse, but all she managed was a wet gurgle that oozed hot blood. Her head bobbed as she fought to look, to know, to keep her blurring vision on Witherwix as it skipped playfully away. Whistling as it plucked a huge colorful circus mallet from where it leaned on the metal riveted wall.

It dragged it along with it as it stalked back to her. The weight of the mallet sent sparks flying as it ground along behind it while the clown made a twisted spectacle of circling Jane like a shark, slitted green eyes mirthful.

"This is a favorite children's game, yes," it giggled as it hefted a mallet, the sight of which made Jain's wrecked insides turn to water while the clown explained the rules of the game like to a child. "You play the piñata. Let's see together, Jane-y, how many whacks it takes to get to the treats inside. Eh? It will be so much fun… For us. It is the Carn-evil way, play, play, play! Haha."

It wildly cackled and swung.

Jane gasped; pain like she'd never known before exploded in her lungs while her ribs cracked, and the clown laughed and laughed. The smashing blow sent her swaying and spinning. Chains clattered and clanked, the fan spun hot air in, and the clown mocked her, pointing and giggling insanely at her bloodied body.

She saw through a blur of tears the clown's awful, rubbery mask-like face stretched into a blood-splattered smile. Its eyes glowed gleefully as its black tongue slithered out, snake-like and forked.

Like a demon.

It lapped the blood, her blood, from its face, and as she spun on the creaking chain, the spattering on its suit and face melted away. The deep red stains from grease-painted face to clown shoes, shrank and shrank until there was no trace of them left. Vanished. Like they had never been there in the first place. But the red paint about its lips *shone brightly*, shiny, like it had just had another fresh coat added to it.

"Mmmm. Jane-y tastes like yummy, stretchy saltwater taffy," It purred.

Then it struck again.

She was crying.

Breathless.

Gagging.

Dying.

All at once.

But not fast enough.

Fast would have been a mercy.

Jane prayed for death as she swayed on the meat hook—and then she saw through the red haze the words on the door, beneath the red glowing *EXIT* sign, a single fat-lettered word scrawled in dripping red paint:

NOWHERE

Shivering, sobbing, Jane gasped for breath that she prayed wouldn't come.

ADMISSION GRANTED

Carnival Way, New York

Abbigail had added Andy's ticket to the wall. She'd tried to guess how many there were. Like guessing how many jellybeans were in a jar for an Easter surprise at church.

Andy had always loved jellybeans.

He adored them.

Particularly the green ones, "cause those are yummy treasures," he would say. He used to hoard the green ones, and she would help him add more and more to his secret stash in his room. She bought the big discount bags during the after-Easter sales and picked them all out one by one to surprise him with a gift.

She wiped a tear from her eyes where she sat outside the room of lament. Sniffed and eyed the bottle of whiskey on the table. She was tempted, but she shook her head, grabbed a Kleenex from the unicorn print box, and got up. Mayor Tallfoot studied her as she headed towards the stairs. "Do you understand now?" he asked as she passed him.

"I know." She stopped. "How many are there in there?"

"I've seen one hundred and twenty tickets delivered and tacked." The little man smiled sadly. "We light candles for them, you know, every Gathering, at night. It's only right, a remembrance. It is, after all, the Carnival Way, our law."

Abbigail didn't know what to say. What laws could clowns and carnies have? How much to charge and how to properly rig and rip people off at the carny-games? Admissions costs? What kind of popcorn should be used? What is the right speed for a tilt-a-whirl spiny ride?

Another thought hit like a punch to the gut. She eyed the door tearfully. "There were a lot more than one hundred and twenty tickets in there."

"I know."

Just then, a cell phone rang, playing that damned carnival pipe organ music. The mayor fumbled with his inside pocket and pulled out a shiny pink smartphone that he put to his ear.

"Yes? … Oh." His face fell, and his head hung. "I see." The light on the screen went dead, and he shook his head as he returned it to his pocket.

"Bobo has died." He withdrew a pink hankey on a string of them all tied together from his other trouser pocket, dabbed his eye, and then stuffed the lot away into his suit jacket pocket.

"I'm sorry," Abbigail offered.

He smiled and nodded. "Your kind condolences, particularly in the face of what you have suffered and will suffer in memory of the lost you hold dear, are most appreciated, Ms. Hobbs." He gestured to the stairs. "Please, it is time to be done here and for you to join the Gathering."

"The Gathering?"

"Oh yes. The big to-do. That's half my job as mayor, to organize the yearly Gathering of the kindred of the carnies and circus folk.

The other half is planning the convention that marks the end of the fun season that our kind lives for. Both are just as big and require a lot of work. The convention, though, that's mostly a huge picnic, a feast, really." Mayor Tallfoot paused. "Don't get me wrong, there're rides and games…because that's who we are and what we do and love, but it's not…" He gestured about with a sigh. "It's not as much *muchness* as it is outside today. But it's still…well, a lot."

"So, it's not always…" Abbigail trailed off as she thought of the wild riot of color and sound that awaited outside.

"A circus?" The little man chuckled. "Yes. And no. Just less so."

"I see." She suddenly very much wanted to leave. She headed up the steps, one by one. Each ringing footfall had a finality to it, like she was nailing shut Andy's coffin, nail by nail, step by step.

"You know…" The mayor asked. "You could join us for more than just the Gathering; most do…"

Abbigail looked back at him.

"It's a way for some," he stared at her, his eyes dark and sad, "to remember what's lost, to be close to them. We've got plenty of places for one such as you…"

"I think I'll pass." Abbigail chuckled. Tears were still hot on her cheeks as she shook her head, trying to picture her and Jane working a cotton candy stand or hawking darts for stuffed bears.

"Are you sure?" the mayor asked. "You know, some believe that by becoming one of us, they can see their lost ones again…one day. We've always room for one more…"

All at once, he seemed like a creepy, pint-sized Circus Jehovah's Witness. Ringing her bell to evangelistically ask if she had a moment to spend with the carnival Christ on high, under the big top.

"No, thank you."

"You're certain?"

"Very." Abbigail replied, all at once feeling a crushing wave of homesickness drowning her, pulling her under the high waters of grief like she was in a rip current. "I just want to go home."

He nodded with sad understanding. "Well, I had to ask, but still, should you change your mind, you know where to find us."

Together, they continued in awkward silence the rest of the way through the clown suit displays lining the hallway leading to the front doors. Abbigail kept her head down, not wanting to look at them, but they all seemed to be watching her.

The sky was turning orange by the time she stepped out into the soupy summer air outside the museum. It hit her in the face like a tennis racket. They were in the process of wheeling Bobo out on a gurney. The old clown looked like he was asleep, strapped in, hands folded over a blanket onto his chest.

"Ah." The mayor sniffed. "Just in time."

Hands brushed him as he was pushed past the crying crowd of clowns, entertainers, and carny folk. Bearded women sobbed, clowns wailed, and carnies raised cans of beer and tearfully toasted his passing. It would have been beautiful if it weren't so damned creepy.

Abbigail watched the procession trail after Bobo the Know-It-All, like he was the Goddamned pope of clowns.

She turned back to the mayor, who stood sniffing and dabbing at his eyes with his string of handkerchiefs. "What are my chances of finding Jane?"

"Jane?"

"The woman I came here with. My guardian—kind of like my mom, I guess." Did she mean that? She guessed she did. Jane may as well have been her new mom, the motherly figure who was there for her when no one else could or would be.

"Your…mom?" the little man asked, squinting.

"Well, not by blood." She smiled. "But by love. She was my

mom's best friend and took me in when…I didn't have anywhere else to go."

"Oh." The mayor sighed. "I didn't realize that was the case."

"What?" Abbigail asked.

"Ah, it's probably nothing, but you should go find her before it's too late." He pointed to the Gathering.

"Too late for *what?*" Worry welled up in her chest again.

"To see the Gathering evening ritual before you leave, of course," he unconvincingly caught himself. "You really should hurry. It's a madhouse here during the Gathering after it gets dark…"

Abbigail sprinted for the tents.

She shouldered roughly through the crowds milling about the many food courts of trucks, carts, booths, and trailers, peddling pretzels, pizza, and anything anyone could imagine. Calling for Jane, screaming her name, but there was no answer.

She was jostled, glared at, and shoved as she pushed through lines and queues of customers, but she hardly noticed. "Jane!" she screamed out, again and again, and all at once, she wanted nothing more than to see Jane and run to her and hug her, squeeze her, and thank her. But she was nowhere to be found.

She ran the gambit through the game alley of dart toss, balloon-popping booths, magnetic fishing games, bowling scams, and water gun horse races. The ear-ringing cacophony of megaphones calling out to pull in gamers, the sounds of the attractions, and the laughs of those playing them drowning her out.

Abbigail searched the big tents next, peeking in, roared at by lions in cages. Trumpeted at by elephants in training circles and cursed at by fist-shaking trainers, but still no Jane.

She did find where they'd taken Bobo, though.

At the very center of the biggest big top, the spotlight shone on him as he lay there in state on his gurney, out on display. Surrounded by mourners, hundreds of them, all humming carnival tunes. Each held a lit candle like they gave out in church on Christmas Eve, complete with the little cardboard ring around it so the hot wax didn't drip on their fingers.

Silently, Abbigail crept back out of that tent. Jane wouldn't have been there. She knew that for a fact. Jane hated wakes. At her mom's, she'd been super fidgety and uncomfortable the whole time, itching to bolt for the exit. And Bobo's… Well, that was just about the creepiest wake she'd ever seen.

Popcorn crunched under her feet as she headed deeper into the field. Colorful tents were everywhere. Yellow and white stripes, red and white, blue and white, black and white. It all blended, mixed up, and mashed together into an overwhelming madhouse of color, sound, and smells. Abbigail wanted to crumple onto her knees on the straw and popcorn scraps and scream her lungs out. But she feared if she did, she would be trampled to death by the delighted denizens of the Gathering as they went about their revelry. Too busy with their ice cream cones and pretzels and prize tickets. None of them saw her.

How could they not see her?

How could they not hear her?

She called for "Mom" and "Jane" interchangeably, over and over. No one so much as blinked. She even grabbed a few to beg them for help, but they just shook her off like she was a discarded slushie cup they had slipped on and walked away.

Then, amid the hubbub, the endless antlike lines of busy, energetic, blurringly colorful movement, running and laughing…a stillness caught her eye.

A lone clown.

All black and white diamonds.

Red pompoms.

A bunch of black balloons floating in a grape-like bunch upon shiny red strings, gathered in the clown's white-gloved hand.

It wasn't just how still the thing was amongst the chaos.

It was the *eyes*.

Those huge, glowing, awful cat eyes piercing her from the deep hollows of its sunken, sharp-lined, painted face.

Unblinking.

Hungry.

Wicked.

She didn't have to wonder who or what because she doubted it was a who, at least in the conventional sense. But whatever else it was, demon or monster, it was also The Golden Ticket Slasher.

Witherwix the clown.

She couldn't move; that terrible green glowing gaze hypnotized her into stony stillness. The more she looked, the more familiar he seemed. And that scared her, the vague sense of having met this thing somewhere before. Or how she knew, deep down in her thundering heart, that it wanted to *help* her in its own sick, twisted way.

Witherwix smiled.

His expression was like an awful parody of a creature whose face didn't work like a human being's should. There was something just slightly off, slightly warped and uncanny. Like what a wretched, evil thing thought a smile should be.

It didn't feel real.

Abbigail's world spun as the demented idea of a clown laughed and smiled and danced around her with its bunch of balloons. Spinning, twirling, whirling…

Then stopped, like a spinney top that flopped over after its spin was done, and she was left breathless, her chest heaving, sweating, and hot, terrified to look away as its horrific, bestial smile got bigger and bigger on its rubbery face. The red lips peeled grotesquely back, and back some more, in ways that sent ice shooting through her innards, grinning like it had a secret to share. From behind its back, it withdrew a bloodied mass of *something*, dangling from its hand by tangles of—hair? Blonde hair. *A head.* The mouth hung open, the milky, glazed eyes wide with terror, the fact smashed in and barely recognizable.

But it was Jane.

The sight cut deep, eviscerating Abbigail, coring her out, slicing her open, and taking the hot, steaming bit that was the last of her family away in its bloody hands.

Abbigail couldn't breathe.

Not properly.

And when she did manage to suck in a breath, it didn't feel like she got any air at all, leaving her gasping, wheezing for the sweet oxygen that the nightmare she was living had sucked out of her.

Witherwix bobbed back and forth as Jane's head swung from its grip, letting loose an insanely raucous laughter that was every pitch of awful and cruel all at once in one booming, shrieking sound.

Abbigail ran.

She only pushed her way back through a few clusters of people before skidding to a stop.

It was in front of her again.

Across the way, staring, holding the head and balloons, smiling excitedly like it was playing a sicko game with her, one for which it was particularly fond.

Abbigail's vision blurred with tears and her belly twisted into knots as she fled again, with the same results. Ten, twenty feet away, it was there, waiting.

Playing.

Toying with her.

Sobbing in a circle of straw that, oddly, not a single of the Gathering's goers entered, as they gave it a wide berth.

Abbigail sank to her knees.

Hands over her face.

Rocking back and forth.

"Hello again, Abb-y," a terrible voice nasally purred as something awful, reeking of stale popcorn, cold hotdogs, sour cotton candy, candy apples, and spoiled beer, all shadowing her in a chilling blackness.

Something heavy dropped to the ground before her and bumped into her leg.

She didn't want to look.

But she did.

Dropping her hands to see Jane's head lying like a discarded soccer ball between her knees, and a pair of massively long red clown shoes shining. Jane stared up at her accusingly.

"This is your fault," the head seemed to scold as the wide, milky eyes reflected Abbigail's horrified face back to her in doubles, like a nightmarish pair of mirrors. *"I tried to warn you. I told you to let it go."*

"Oh…God," Abbigail gasped. "I'm so sorry, I'm sorry, I'm so sorry… Oh God, Jane… Mom, I'm so sorry…"

She looked up, sobbing, her eyes burning with tears that poured from them like she was a leaky faucet as she outwardly shook. And inwardly, she spun like a carousel, staring at the world through a blurred, tormented twisting. She was so terrified that she was frozen stiff. Unable to so much as scream.

"The price is paid." Each word puffed the acrid stink of sweetness and saltiness and savory delights in a gust of hot breath. "Admission is made." It held out a hand to her, and in it appeared a golden ticket, shining and metallic, even in Witherwix's shadow.

She remembered.

It came in a hot, dizzying rush.

The Wicked Woods.

Witherwix.

Andy.

She had wanted to join him.

And somehow, Witherwix had decided to oblige her.

"Take it, Abb-y." It lowered the ticket to offer it.

She shook her head.

"TAKE IT!" it bellowed, and she fell over, curled in a ball, her world shattered, her mind breaking. "Aww… Abb-y needs a nappy. Poor, poor, happy, kindly Abb-y," it sang as it reached down, lifting her effortlessly by the ankle and holding her up before it. "Witherwix will care for her. Yes, yes, we shall."

It reached into its pocket and drew out a sack that had *100% high grade, all-natural popcorn kernels* printed in faded letters along its wide burlap front. Abbigail felt like a rat caught by its tail, squeaking and terrified and wriggling as the big, bad man was about to toss it in a bucket of water to drown it. She was too scared to speak, too scared to beg.

Abbigail whimpered.

She cried and sobbed.

She even wet herself.

But Witherwix just looked at her like she was silly, shaking his head as he hovered her over the sack's mouth. "In you go, Abb-y. Nappy time on the way to Super Happy Fun Land. An-dy is waiting. He just cannot wait to play with you and show you all his new favorite games!"

Witherwix stuffed her inside, and she was falling, dropped, spinning in darkness forever, her screams shrill and echoing as down, down, down she went.

THE GOLDEN TICKET

Super Happy Fun Land – Everywhere

Abb-y squealed with fun time happiness while she tumbled out of the sack. It had smelled absolutely, wonderfully delicious, with a capital D, like popping corn, hot and fresh. She was up and smiling as her clown friend grinned broadly and brightly back at her.

"Ah, there you are, our perfect, sweet, pretty, kindly Abb-y. Our friend. We were afraid we'd lost you."

"Silly." Abb-y giggled. "I was in a sack on your back. You couldn't lose me. Friends don't lose best friends."

"Oh, so true." Witherwix laughed as he bent at the hip to her tiny height with his white-gloved hands on his hips. "I have a super surprise, Abb-y, all for you, fresh, shiny, and good."

"Really?" She loved surprises. And to her ears, this sounded like it was the bestest surprise of them all in the whole widest of worlds.

"Would you like to see?" the silly clown asked.

"Boy, would I!"

From his sleeve, he produced a golden ticket. It was so pretty and just as shiny as he had promised, 'cause clowns were friends, and friends never lied. He handed it to her, and she took it in both her tiny mittened hands.

It was warm.

The heat pleasantly bled through her mittens' pink woolen knitting. It was comforting, hot, and soothing. Like holding a cup of hot cocoa on a chilly night. The reflection of her cherubic face shimmered in it like a mirror. The face, her face reflected at her, had a super big smile on her blue, pudgy, little pouting lips. It laughed and waved at her; it was silly. It was wonderful; it was the bestest of magic.

"It's perfect." She gasped while tearing up with joy. "Thank you so much, Witherwix. You really and truly are my bestest friend forever and ever!"

"Aww. Aren't you cute and sweet? We could just eat you all up." The clown offered his hand. Then together they walked on top of the snow across a wide field, like a moat between the trees and the hugeness of a place the likes of which she had never seen. The music and laughter grew louder and louder the closer they got.

It felt like the cold dawn before Christmas morning, excitement bubbling up as the chill sent shivers of anticipation through her. The happy moon's glow washed over the snowy expanse, making it shimmer pearly white and reflecting the flashing lights, sparkling like heaps of jewels that excited the eyes.

The joy of it…

It was beyond words.

Beyond understanding.

She stared, her eyes gleaming and huge with wonder.

Roller coasters rumbled, screams of laughter filled the air, and a big Ferris wheel, the biggest ever, lit up the night as it spun. It all poked up out of a colorfully striped canvas wall that fenced it all in, wall-like, like a play fort with pillows and blankets. The smells were upon the wind now, too, strong and yummy.

Oh, the smells…

Abb-y couldn't wait to taste what smelled so good, all of it. Each-and-every bite. She laughed as she strode along to the snow dunes, staring happily ahead.

They reached the entrance, a huge, colorful, shiny, plasticky castle. Flags flew from its towers, and its gate was a happy clown face with the funniest spiny propeller hat she had ever seen. And huge red eyes that clicked and went this way and that like it was watching. All the while, it boomingly, like deep rumbles of thunder, laughed and laughed over the music and noise from the games, rides, and fun emanating from beyond its toothy gates.

Just past the mouth, almost hidden by its big blocky teeth, was a group of children. All in bright colors, smiling big, blue-lipped smiles as one in the front jumped up and down and waved. He was tiny, blond, and his eyes were brimming with tears of joy as he called to her, "Abb-y, Abb-y, come on, hurry, we've got so much to show you: bouncy houses, funhouses, candy houses. Rides and games, oh, Abb-y, you must hurry!"

"Hi, An-dy!" she called out, jumping up and down with energy like she was on a pogo stick and waving, "Hi!"

"Hi!" he hollered back. "I missed you!"

Abb-y frowned. She had missed him, too. She only just remembered that. It made her sad, so super, sobby sad to remember, and then it was gone. He was there; no more need for tears. Ever, ever again.

From then on out, it was going to be ice cream smiles, roller coaster squeals, and jumpy house jollies. And no one there to say it was time to go home, or it was time to go beddy-bye.

"I missed you too!" she called to An-dy, and those words were like a super warm hug to them both.

Witherwix waved to An-dy, then to the admission booth—a sugar-frosted and gum-dropped gingerbread guard tower. Which was, of course, manned by another happy clown with red makeup circles about his friendly eyes who joyfully waved to her and Witherwix.

"Go on, Abb-y. Witherwix will follow after soon."

"Are you sure?" she asked.

"Of course." Witherwix smiled. "We are always here, waiting, watching, playing. We will have such fun together, all of us. But you must go to them, to An-dy, as we have more playmates to bring you. We promise we will be along soon, and that is when the real fun begins."

That was enough for Abb-y.

A clown's word was his bond.

And this clown was her clown.

Her bestest friend.

Abb-y ran off with a squeal of delight and made her way to the gumdrop-studded gingerbread admission booth with her shiny golden ticket outstretched.

"Hi-ya there, Abb-y, I'm Bobo the Know-It-All, and it's my pleasure to welcome you to Super Happy Fun Land." The clown grinned from behind his cage window as she slid in her ticket. He punched it and handed it back. "Have a wonderful ever-after of play, Abb-y, enjoy the games an' food an' fun."

The ticket now had a smiley face with her name on it in a circle—then it was gone. Lost in golden sparkles like fireflies that popped and fizzed like a sparkler on the Fourth of July.

An-dy was calling her.

She ran to him, jumping over the big teeth of the clown's head, and wrapped her arms tightly about him. They spun about and giggled as he introduced his friends. Who were now her friends, too. They all had such big, nice smiles and such big, shiny teeth. And all of them were super-duper ice cream sundae sweet. Abbigail paused and looked back to wave to Witherwix. She was so happy. She had never felt such joy. Truthfully, she was starting to forget anything but what joy felt like, as it warmed her up like pizza bites spinning on a microwave heater plate.

Witherwix smiled and waved to her, then began to lift off the ground. Pulled up, up, up, and up some more by a bunch of shiny black balloons that reminded her of grapes with red strings. Amazing! Where had the balloons come from? It must have been clown magic. Abb-y watched with wonder as Witherwix the clown, *her clown*, drifted higher into the sky. Higher and higher. Laughing and waving as the teeth came crashing down on the clown-headed entry to Super Happy Fun Land.

CONTENT WARNINGS

Please note: it should be assumed that basic horror tropes will apply. These include death, gore, and violence.

graphic violence

attempted sexual assault

kidnapping/loss of a child

Я.R. Harrow is a prolific on-spectrum reader and writer from the rural Adirondack regions of New York State. The former seminarian is the son of Scottish Immigrants, who developed an early fondness for the classics and especially horror, a passion that followed him throughout his adult life as he faced many harsh challenges and realities. Which culminated in his eventual medical disablement and retirement from coaching, and volunteer firefighting. Now, he dedicates his time between work and family, finding the time to invest in his lifelong passion, writing.

linktr.ee/RRHARROW

THANK YOU!

Thank you for supporting Graveside Press and our authors. One of the biggest ways you can help is to leave a star rating or a review wherever you purchased your copy!

Stay spooky.

graveside-press.com